The Sherlock Holmes Adventure

THE SHERLOCK HOLMES ADVENTURE

Regis McCafferty

With Warm Regards

Regis Eric Cafferty

iUniverse, Inc.
New York Lincoln Shanghai

The Sherlock Holmes Adventure

All Rights Reserved © 2004 by Regis McCafferty

No part of this book may be reproduced or transmitted in any form or by any means, graphic, electronic, or mechanical, including photocopying, recording, taping, or by any information storage retrieval system, without the written permission of the publisher.

iUniverse, Inc.

For information address:
iUniverse, Inc.
2021 Pine Lake Road, Suite 100
Lincoln, NE 68512
www.iuniverse.com

ISBN: 0-595-31547-X

Printed in the United States of America

*Dedicated to Phil Bradford
Friend, Aficionado of the Pipe
And a True Gentleman*

Contents

FOREWORD ix
THE CASE OF THE MUMBLING MUM 1
THE BRADLEY BLEND AFFAIR 8
THE AMESBURY AFFAIR 20
THE SHERLOCK HOLMES ADVENTURE 50
THE KENDAL AFFAIR 87
THE CASE OF THE GLASGOW HORROR 116

FOREWORD

Three of the Joshua Pitt adventures in this group of short stories were previously published in 2003 as part of a mixed collection titled, *Then...Now...Whenever...* including the title story of this collection. At the urging of friends and readers, however, I have added three more unpublished stories featuring Joshua Pitt, Victorian inquiry agent, and present them to you here as a group. They are intended to celebrate the era of gaslight, England before the turn of the twentieth century, and most of all, the genre of detection brought to us by Sir Arthur Conan Doyle through his inimitable Sherlock Holmes.

Joshua Pitt is a young man who stands in awe of Sherlock Holmes and conducts his investigations in the shadow of the great detective. As much as possible, I have tried to be factual with locations, the language of the times, and in particular the sights, sounds, and idiosyncrasies, of Victorian London. I hope I have been moderately successful.

Regis McCafferty
2004

THE CASE OF THE MUMBLING MUM

Her hat led her through his office door—a small red hat, set askew and dominated by wilted yellow flower. Whether the flower was real or not, he couldn't tell. She looked slightly disheveled and out of breath from the walk up three flights of stairs. Dumpy, wearing an assortment of clothes that looked as if they'd been pulled out of a bag in the dark, she paused, taking in the room until her eyes finally came to rest on Joshua Pitt.

"Ere now, you that private inquiry agent wot finds people an things like 'at?"

"Aye, Lass, sometimes. Won't you have a seat Miss…?"

"Molly Brick, like in brick."

"Well Miss Brick, just have…" but she was already flopping into the chair across from his desk.

"You say someone is missing?"

"Me Mum. One minute she was there, the next, gone. Quick as a fart, it was."

"And where was it she disappeared from?"

"Regent's Park. Just an hour ago."

"Did the police…?"

"Don' want no coppers. Not as they'd care much anyway. She were a Dollymop wot dint work for no Cash Carrier, did she? But a while back, she lost all her teeth. She mumbled then, Mum did. Pickups couldn't understand enough to agree on a price…or the menu."

Pitt followed her easily enough, though her dialect was a mix of cockney and East End slang. Molly Brick's mother was a prostitute that didn't work for a pimp. She freelanced, as most did, but when she lost her teeth it became difficult to negotiate a price for her services. Pitt suspected cheap Gin contributed to the problem as well. He also suspected Molly had followed in her mother's footsteps.

"You were with her in the park?"

"I were. We was sittin' on a bench talkin' over how bad business has been, when she said she wanted a cuppa from one of those Ducketts wot sells from carts. She stepped around a curve in the pathway. I waited a few minutes—couldn't see because of the bushes, could I? Then went to look, but no Mum. I ast the Duckett and he hadn't seed her. Wunt but fifty feet or so. She wuntna gone somewhere without tellin' me, now would she?"

Pitt picked up a pipe from a large, shallow bowl that held several, lit it, and took several puffs. "What part of the Park were you in?"

"Near the lake loop, past Hanover Gate."

"That's wooded and there's a lot of shrubbery. Did you search around?"

"Ahrrr…that's wot took an hour, dint it? What with all them attacks on women this week gone, I got scared…"

Pitt was surprised to see her near tears. He sat his pipe on the desk and stared past her, thinking it over.

"I charge five pounds for the first day and that includes expenses. After that it's two pounds a day, plus expenses."

"Five thickers! Take me two days to earn one thicker!"

"That's what I charge and I'll go with you now to Regents Park."

She fished around in her bag, grumbling, head bobbing to the point that he thought the flower would fall from he hat to his desk. Finally, she found a little leather purse, fished some more and deposited a fiver on his desk. He took the money, slipped it inside his top desk drawer, locked it, and picked up the pipe from his desktop.

"Let's take a look around the Park."

They left the building, Joshua pausing to light his pipe, and walked toward Regents, Molly still mumbling about the five pounds. This was Joshua's second case, having only been in business for little more than three weeks. The first had been a simple one involving a butcher's wife, though it had led to murder.

Joshua was born in Glasgow, Scotland and lived there until age 12 when his father died. He and his mother then moved to London on the promise that she would have a job as a seamstress, but the job turned out to be slaving in a sweatshop making uniforms for nurses, waitresses, maids and such. He continued his schooling and she worked, but when he was 16 she died of consumption and he took to the streets, sometimes running with a ragamuffin gang of boys known as the Baker Street Irregulars. When not stealing from carts or picking an easy pocket, they did odd jobs for a consulting detective named Sherlock Holmes. He enjoyed that—it was an adventure and Mr. Holmes paid fairly for a job well done.

He went from job to job, never holding a position for longer than it took to become boring to him, usually less than six months. At 25, he landed a job on a packet freighter out of London that made regular voyages to Cork, Dublin, Glasgow and back to London. He stuck with it for two years, earning a reputation as a hard worker and problem solver. He had an analytical mind, a vivid imagination, and seemed to find solutions to many problems when others could not. It was one such instance when he managed to discover why the ship's log had disappeared, that the Captain suggested he'd do well as a detective.

The suggestion stuck with him and for more than a year, he saved all he could from his pay, his only luxury being three Peterson pipes from Fox Tobacconists in Grafton Street when they docked in Dublin and he went ashore. He would occasionally purchase tobacco there, but most often waited till he returned to London to buy one of the Gawith blends at Lewis Tobacconists, 19 St. James Street. Then he would wander for several hours or more in the Strand, puffing merrily away at his pipe, and looking in shop windows at things he couldn't afford before walking back to his small bed-sitting room west of Regent's Park.

Finally, in early summer, 1895 he rented rooms at 22C Baker Street that would serve as office, sitting room and bedroom. Being on the third floor had advantages and disadvantages. It was above the street, quieter, and offered an occasional breeze in the summer, but his clients had to walk up three floors to engage him. Still, it served well for a beginning.

They entered the park at Hanover Gate, crossed the outer circle road and walked along the path that bridged the northern neck of the boating lake. After crossing the second footbridge, Molly pointed to a path running off to the left and a small bench just beyond.

"That's where I last saw me Mum. We was on that bench and she went round that bend and bushes for a cuppa."

They walked around the bend in the path and standing in a shallow alcove under a tree was a vendor's cart attended by a Duckett, as Molly called him. As they approached, he looked up and seeing Molly Brick, said, "See 'ear, I tole you afore, I dint set eyes on your Mum, if that's wot you drug this gent along for."

"We'd like two cups of tea, please." Pitt laid a shilling on the top of the cart.

The vendor squinted, paused, then poured tea into two old ceramic mugs. Before he could reach for the shilling to make change, Pit laid two more shillings on the cart top but kept his hand on them. "Was there a man, then, who walked past here a few minutes before Miss Brick came asking about her mother? Maybe about the same time as her mother came for a cup of tea?"

"I don' pay no mind, less they buy tea or cakes."

"Who was the man who bought something from you before Miss Brick came asking about her mother?"

"Dint say there was a man."

As Pitt started to pick up the shillings, the Vendor said, "Old Eddie…But 'e's a nice old cove. Wuntna hurt nobody."

"Did he just buy a cuppa?"

"Had a tea and cake, din't he? Said he'd sold an old sailor's locker and made a couple o' quid. Leastways, tha's wot I understood 'im to say."

"And where does Old Eddie live?"

The vendor was silent a moment, not wanting to give anything up on a friend. Pitt slipped another shilling from his pocket, set it on top of the first three, and pushed them forward.

"E's got rooms in that old row in Siddons Lane, dun't he?"

"Does Eddie have a last name?"

"Fast. Old Eddie Fast."

Pitt took his hand from the shillings and they disappeared. He pulled his pipe from his pocket, lit it, and turned to Molly. "It's a start, anyway. I think we should have a talk with Old Eddie."

They began walking back toward Hanover Gate and had taken a dozen steps when Pitt stopped. "Wait here, Miss Brick." He turned and went back to the vendor, spoke with him for a moment, and then returned to Molly.

"Did 'e know somethin' else, then?"

"Maybe. We'll see in a few minutes."

They walked out of the Park and followed Outer Circle Road south toward Baker Street. Siddons was a short, one block lane that ran parallel to Baker Street and contained several row houses.

They made an odd pair as they walked. Her dress and hip movement wouldn't necessarily have labeled her as a prostitute but it wouldn't have surprised anyone either. He, on the other hand, was dressed in a tweed coat, grey trousers and Jodhpur shod—very upper middle class looking though he certainly wasn't. He was taller than average, slightly under six feet, well built, with neatly trimmed deep auburn hair and beard. His build, he got from his father who was a tall man, and the color of his hair from his mother. Walking together, they drew occasional knowing smiles from some of the men they passed, and he suspected, from some of the women too, but they hid it well.

They turned onto Baker Street, walked to the end of the block and turned right on Melcome Street for a short block to Siddons Lane, a short street of shops, taverns, apartments and bedsitting rooms.

Joshua stopped in front of a tavern called *The Gamecock* and turned to Molly. "Would you like a drink, Miss Brick?"

"Well, now…"

"It comes out of expenses."

"Could be usin' a small tot…"

They entered the tavern and took a seat in the corner. The landlord looked them over, frowned when his eyes rested on Molly, took one last swipe at the bar with his rag and came over to the table.

Before he could open his mouth, Joshua said, "A half pint of Guinness for myself and a tot of gin for the lady."

The landlord flipped the rag over his shoulder, turned, muttering something about "lady" and went back to the bar. Pitt excused himself and followed. He leaned against the bar and watched the landlord draw the Guinness.

"You know a fellow named Fast? Old Eddie Fast?"

"What you want him for?"

"Just talk—nothing more. I'm trying to locate someone the lady knows."

"Lady…Fook!"

"Yes…well, be that as it may, I'd still like to talk with Eddie. We were told he lives on this street somewhere. It would save time knocking on doors if you could help us out." As he talked, he laid a half crown on the bar.

The coin disappeared under the rag. "You'll be trying the boarding house three doors down. I didn't say, did I?"

"I don't know you." Pitt picked up the drinks and went back to the table.

"Ask the landlord, did you?" Molly put half her gin away in a gulp.

"We'll try the boarding house a couple of doors away." He took a sip of Guinness, pulled his pipe from his pocket, then tamped and lit it. He told Molly he suspected her mother had managed to connect with Eddie Fast. All the pieces were there. They were in the same place at the same time and Eddie had a bit of money made from a recent sale. The other telling reason, he'd keep to himself for now. For Molly's "Mum" it might have been a case of a quick sale or no sale, which would explain why she hadn't taken the time to return to the bench where Molly was sitting.

They finished their drinks, left *The Gamecock* and walked half a block to the boarding house. A small sign penned, Rooms To Let, was pinned to the door. Pitt turned the bell crank. After a moment, the door was opened by a short, stout woman wearing an apron and pushing ragged cropped hair out of her eyes. She looked them over, her eyes working Molly from head to toe.

"No short term rooms," she said and started to close the door.

Pitt stepped forward, putting his hand on the door. "We're not needing a room, Misses. We'd like to see Mr. Fast."

"What you wanting Old Eddie for?"

"I need some help locating someone and I think Mr. Fast can help."

"Well, he's busy now, in't he?"

Pitt suspected as much and with some effort, stifled a smile. "Please be so kind as to tell Mr. Fast *and his guest* that Miss Brick is here. I think he'll see us."

She looked them over again and without a word, opened the door for them to step inside. She started up the stairs, and then paused, sniffing the air. "I have some scones in the oven," she said, stepping down. "He's third floor, first door on the right."

By the time they reached the third floor landing, Molly was blowing hard and her hat had reached a precarious and rakish angle. If possible, the yellow flower looked even more wilted. Joshua paused, giving her a chance to get her wind, then tapped at the door. He heard sounds and voices but no one came to the door. He rapped harder, heard a giggle, and a gravelly voice said, "Whatcher want?" Then quieter, obviously to someone else inside, "Nosey ole bitch!" Pitt was sure Old Eddie was referring to the landlady.

"Molly Brick and friend to see you Mr. Fast."

"Jasus!" A woman's voice inside.

The door opened a few inches and a partially bald head and unshaven face appeared. He looked them up and down and mumbled something Pitt could barely make out but took it to mean he was asking what their business was. As Pitt had surmised, Old Eddie Fast didn't have any teeth. He started to ask if Eddie's guest was Molly's mother when Molly barged past, shoving open the door and knocking Eddie out of the way.

"Mum!"

Sitting on a disheveled bed, naked from the waist up and making no attempt to cover herself, was an older version of Molly Brick. In one hand she held an unlit cheroot and a half filled glass of what Pitt took to be gin in the other.

"Wadda fook you doon 'er daater?"

"I been lookin' for ya Mum, haven't I? You went gone from the Park."

"Offer ta gin," Eddie chimed in.

And that's not all, thought Pitt, smiling. "Well, we've found your mother, Miss Brick. I'll leave you to talk over family matters." Or maybe a threesome, he mused, if Old Eddie has enough money. As he turned toward the door, Molly grabbed his arm.

"I'll be thankin' you Mr. Pitt, won't I? Don' know how you knew to be lookin' here for 'er, but thank you just the same."

"You're welcome, Miss Brick. I'm just glad she's come to no harm."

As he walked back to Baker Street it was beginning to cloud over and there was a slight cooling of the air. As he always did when he finished a case, he'd write up the particulars in his notebook, though this one was simple enough. The solution, of course, lay in the comment made by the vendor in Regent's Park, "Leastways, tha's wot I understood 'im to say." Pitt returned to ask if by any chance Old Eddie didn't have any teeth. When the vendor, or Duckett as Molly called him, told Pitt that Eddie hadn't had any teeth as long as he'd known him, he assumed that Molly's "Mum" and Eddie spoke the same language. They could understand each other. Eddie had some extra money and "Mum" had something to sell. It was only a matter of tracking Eddie down.

Fog tonight, he thought, as he paused to light his pipe. A good night for a small fire in the fireplace, some hot tea, and a wee dram of whiskey.

END

THE BRADLEY BLEND AFFAIR

Having just finished tea and scones, Joshua Pitt was still relaxing in his robe and lighting the first pipe of the day when there was a knock at his sitting room door. Thinking it was his landlady come after the breakfast tray, he bade her come in. It was Mrs. Keating, but she was immediately followed by Michael Byrne, better known as Mick, who was senior clerk at Bradley Tobacconists of Oxford Street and one of the best tobacconists in London. Though he was not an easily rattled fellow, it could be seen he was in an agitated state. His soft gillie hat was tilted at a rakish angle as if an afterthought, and his white beard, usually neat and distinguished, was unkempt and uncombed.

"Mr. Pitt, I need your help."

Pitt came around his desk and with his hand on Mick's arm, guiding him to one of the wingbacks near the fireplace. "Please sit down, Mick. The tea is still hot under the cozy unless you'd like something stronger, or both."

"Both, I think."

"Both it is then." He walked to the sideboard, poured a small tot of brandy in a glass and handed it to Mick with a cup of tea. He tossed off the brandy and then leaned back in the chair as he took a sip of tea.

"Now, my friend," Pitt said as he picked up my pipe to relight it, "tell me what the problem is and how I can be of assistance."

"They're missing! Gone! Both of them!"

"Who is missing, Mick?"

"Not who, Mr. Pitt—what!"

"Mister is too formal Mick, just Pitt will do, or Joshua if you like. Now calm down, start from the beginning and tell me what's missing. Would you like another brandy?"

"No, no thank you. This tea is just fine."

He took a sip, set the cup on the table between the chairs, and fished through his pockets for a pipe and tobacco. Finding both, he proceeded to fill and light a pipe before beginning his tale.

"I don't know if you stopped by the shop last August, but if you did, you will remember that I was gone for a few days at that time. You would have been told I was on holiday, and in a manner of speaking, that was correct...so far as it went. In truth, I spent several days in Jarnac, France, at Chaueau de Courvoisier, making arrangements for a quantity of aged cognac and two quite old but sound oaken barrels. In the company of both cognac and barrels, I then traveled to the Jersey Islands and the home of Thomas Aubin and Philip Germain, tobacco blenders of the highest order, who's premises face the harbour of St. Helier on the coast.

"It was our intention, at Bradley's of Oxford Street, to have a special tobacco blended that would be available only at our store for the Christmas season. It combined sweet sun cured tobaccos with aged Virginia tobaccos, blended with a touch of Turkish and Syrian. To this mixture was added a mist of Courvoisier before being layered, pressed, sliced, and then packed in the oak barrels to age for two months. The barrels were delivered yesterday, and Bradley's Christmas Blend, as we named it, was to go on sale the last day of November, which is Monday, three days hence. This morning, however, when I went to the store early to finish our pre-season inventory, the barrels were gone!

"More to the point, my chance to become part owner in the store is likely gone with them. As you know, Ian Fairbanks, the sole owner, is getting on in years and is less and less hands on, as it were. The Christmas blend was my idea and he agreed, though reluctantly because of the cost—not only of the blend itself, but of the trip I made to the continent and to the Jersey Islands. He said, however, that if it proved to be a profitable venture, he would consider making me a partner after the first of the year. For more than ten years, it has been my dream to have my own shop and I saw a partnership in Bradley's as a proper step in that direction—perhaps even full ownership in a few years. Now, I may be lucky to retain my position at Bradley's after Mr. Fairbanks comes in this evening and learns the tobacco has been stolen."

Pitt sat quietly during Mick's narrative, listening closely, but at the same time mentally forming questions he might ask.

"Tell me, Mick, apart from yourself, and Mr. Fairbanks on some evenings, who else works in the shop?"

"Well, there's Basil Lewis, also full time, but you don't see him in the store proper much. He's content to maintain the stock, place orders for cigars and tobacco, and mix the store blends we sell. He also does any pipe repairs we get from time to time. We do have a new part-time lad named Kevin Wallace, who's been with us about four weeks and will provide additional help through the holiday season. Nice lad, originally from Woolmet, near Edinburgh I think, and very interested in the tobacco business."

"And after the holidays?"

"What do you mean?"

"After the holiday season, will Kevin be retained?"

"I believe Mr. Fairbanks promised him work through the second week of January. It is only a temporary position, you see."

"Who knew about the Christmas blend? I mean the details: where you went, when you would be back, the nature of the blend."

"Everyone at the shop knew we'd have a special blend this year, but as to the details, they were kept between Fairbanks and myself, though we've begun to tell customers that we'd have a very special and exclusive blend for the holiday season. But only Fairbanks and myself knew the barrels had been delivered and were stored in the shop. There'd been no opportunity to tell the others."

"I see... What size barrels were they?"

"Both were thirteen gallon."

"And how were they marked?"

"They were brandy barrels and stamped as such, but they had our shipping labels on them as well."

"Well, finish your tea while I get dressed and I'll return to the shop with you. It must be almost opening time."

"Yes, yes it is, in about thirty minutes."

"Plenty of time. We can be there in twenty minutes or less."

After dressing, Pitt slipped into his ulster and wool cap, pocketed a pipe and tobacco pouch, and picked up his blackthorn stick on the way out the door. It was cold. Cold with a bite that took one's breath, though a weak sun shone through the typical winter haze of London. They walked briskly and were in front of Bradley's in little more than ten minutes. Mick let them in with his key, turned up the gaslight, and made for the stove at the back of the shop to light a coal fire. Pitt took the opportunity to look at the pipes in the front case, seeing several he'd like to look closer at, but one in particular—a large straight GBD billiard caught his eye. Well, plenty of time for that later. He walked to the rear of the shop where Mick was just putting a match to the tinder beneath the coal in the stove.

Mick turned to Pitt. "It's a lovely, wee stove and we'll have the chill off in no time. Come to the back and I'll show you where I left the kegs of tobacco."

They walked through a curtained doorway, past an alcove that held scales and containers for mixing tobaccos, to a section near the rear door that had shelves of pipes and a workbench for making repairs. Mick pointed to a small wooden skid on the floor next to the bench. "They were sitting right there when I closed the shop last evening."

"You were the last one out, then?"

"Aye. Basil finished mixing some blends about mid evening and went home to supper and family. Kevin finished sweeping up, checked to make sure everything was secure here in the back room, and left right at closing time."

"Did you check to see that the back door was bolted?"

"I could see that the drop bar was in place, and of course, I locked the front door on my way out. The front door was locked when I arrived this morning and the drop bar still in place at the back. I looked, but there was no sign either door had been forced and being in the middle of the block, we have no windows other than the small displays at the front of the shop."

Pitt took his pipe from his pocket, tamped and lit it, then walked to the back door to look closely at the drop bar. It was a stout piece of iron a bit less than an inch thick and fifteen inches long with a two-inch leg bent ninety degrees at the top. The door, when closed, had two iron eyes six inches apart that fitted in place an inch below two matching iron eyes bolted to the door frame. To secure the door, one only had to run the drop bar vertically from the top through all four eyes. It was held in place by it's own weight and the bend at the top kept it from falling through. Simple, effective, and strong enough that the door would have to be torn from its hinges before it would give.

There was no indication of forced entry but Pitt spent a couple of minutes looking closely at the bar, paying particular attention to the top at the bend, and sliding it up and down several times. He then moved a stepstool to the door and inspected the top of the door, giving special attention to the leading top edge where the door closed against the frame. Finally, he stepped down, put the stool back near the skid, then opened the door and walked out into the alleyway. He walked up and down the alley about twenty feet or so, stopping once to examine several wooden crates stacked against the back of the building, and then returned to look closely at the door just below the iron door ring. Mick watched from the doorway without saying a word. Pitt stepped inside, followed by Mick who closed and secured the door, and then walked to the front of the shop. He paused in front of the display case and looked again at the pipes.

"That's a nice GBD you have there, Mick."

"Mr. Pitt, if you can get my tobacco back, you can have your pick of any pipe in the shop!"

Pitt smiled as he picked up a small box of matches from the counter. "Just out of curiosity, where did Kevin work before he came here?"

"He once mentioned working at the *Black Dog* near the Cider Cellars in Maiden Lane behind the Strand, a public house with a reputation of less than sterling character, or so I've heard. It's a place frequented by the fast, young swells of the City and West End after the theaters are closed. Directly before coming here though, he clerked at Twinings in the Strand, but said he saw no future for himself in the tea business. But he's an ambitious lad, always on the lookout for an extra shilling or two."

Pitt, lighting his pipe, mumbled around the stem, "Thought as much."

"What was that?"

"Nothing," said Pitt, "just talking to myself. I'm going to leave for a while but should be back before noon. Don't mention the missing tobacco to anyone, but if Lewis or Wallace ask about the kegs, just say something to the effect that Mr. Fairbanks must have picked them up."

"You have an idea, then, of what happened or who took them?"

"An idea, yes, but no more than that for the time being. All is conjecture at this point and I need more information before we can act. One thing though…"

"Yes?"

"Put that GBD Billiard behind the counter. I'll be wanting a closer look when I get back." Smiling, he walked out the door and down Oxford Street in search of a cab.

The ride to New Scotland Yard was little more than ten minutes and on a warmer day, he probably would have walked. As it was, he sat in the corner on the pedestrian side of the cab, puffing on his pipe and watching early morning London—the London he never tired of—slide by the window. He was not a world traveler, but had visited any number of large cities on the continent as well as the British Isles. Some were boring, dirty, and foul, while others were bright, interesting, and fresh—yet with none of them did he have the passionate love affair he had with London. The physical aspects of London ran the gamut from indescribably filthy to splendid elegance, but for Pitt, it was not so much physical London that captured him, it was the state of mind—that unexplainable, prepossessing quality exhibited in the steadfast determination of her people to endure and improve. To be sure, many were simply *living it through* as some poet said, but even the whores who plied their trade in the streets for bed and bread, wanted something more, whether they succeeded or not.

Arriving at the Yard, he paid off the cabbie and entered the building, intending to see Inspector MacLeish if he was available or Inspector Bell if he was not. He found MacLeish, feet propped on his desk, unlit pipe in mouth, deeply engrossed in something in the *Morning Chronicle*.

Pitt entered quietly and in a deep, loud voice, said, "Would the Inspector be liking a Guinness while he relaxes with the newspaper?"

MacLeish's feet came down with a bang and he sat bolt-upright, turning toward Pitt as he did. "Jasus, lad, don' do that! Me heart goddam near gave out."

Pitt laughed and strode across the room with his hand out. "Has the criminal element gone to Brighton or are you just contemplating retirement?"

"Neither, laddie. Just havin' a quick look-see at ta agony columns. There be a wealth of information here, as well ya know."

"That I do, Mac, that I do. They've pointed me in the right direction more than once."

"So…what'd be bringin' ya ta the Yard?"

"Tobacco."

"Tobacco? Well, if tis a bowl you'd be wantin'…" MacLeish reached for a pouch near an ashtray with two pipes in it.

"No, stolen tobacco. Bradley's Christmas blend seems to have disappeared last night from their locked and bolted shop. It's an expensive blend that was the result of a trip to the continent, and to Auben-Germain, tobacco blenders on the Jersey's. It was stored in two thirteen gallon Courvoisier kegs."

"If they file a report wi' us, we'll look to it."

"An' tha's the rub, as you're fond of saying. Mick persuaded the shop owner, a reluctant Mr. Fairbanks, that a special high-grade blend would be good for holiday business. But if it's truly lost, Mick is convinced his job may be in jeopardy as well as any future prospects. I'd like your assistance but would prefer to keep it a non-police matter."

"Aye, well…if all were locked as ya say, tis havin' the mark of an inside job."

Pitt fished his pipe from his pocket, tamped with his forefinger and lit it. "That's what I think, and in fact, I have a suspect. Here's what I think happened…"

For the next five minutes, Pitt laid out a probable scenario based on his investigation at the shop, and what needed to be done to recover the tobacco. When he finished, he leaned back in his chair and drew on his pipe. "Well, what do you think?"

"Tis proper soundin' for sure. We 'ave 'ad cases of mistaken identity afore but ne'er tobacco. I take it you'd like me tae accompany you—lend an official air so tae speak."

"That I would, and I think we can arrange for a pint of Guinness."

"Alright, laddie. I will tell Bell tae cover me for a couple hours."

The stifling aroma of gin, beer, smoke, and the reek of sweat hit them as they pushed open the door to the Black Dog, a dirty, underground tavern in Maiden Lane. Bad as it was, it was still patronized by middle class theater-goers and young men with a few pounds in their purse looking for a cheap prostitute. This early in the day, however, it was those hard pressed for a tot of gin or a beer that were standing at the counter, and a few haggard faces turned in their direction for a moment, then back to their drink. Pitt walked to the bar, MacLeish at his shoulder, and ordered two Guinness. When the barkeep returned, Pitt took a sip of his stout and asked for the proprietor.

"Who'd be asking for 'im, then?"

"Pitt, Joshua Pitt."

"What be yer business?"

"That's between him and me."

"He be in the back room, but you'll nowt be seein' 'im till I know why." He slipped his hands under the edge of the counter, but whether for a gun or belaying pin, Pitt had no way of knowing.

MacLeish stepped forward and shoved his warrant card in the man's face. "Both hands tae bar lest ya want tae be wearin' darbys. An' if you reach for tha' pull bell tae warn the boss, I'll be breakin' both your bloody hands." He glanced at Pitt and nodded toward the rear. Pitt headed for the room at the back with MacLeish following a few steps behind.

Pitt entered the room without knocking. Seated behind a very large, very old desk, was a very big man of damn near twenty stone, if Pitt was any judge. He was completely bald but with a thick handlebar mustache, and if he had any neck, it was lost in the jowls that sagged into his collar. He made no move, nor showed surprise, but looked directly past Pitt to MacLeish.

"It has been a while, Angus," he said with a trace of a grin.

It was MacLeish who showed surprise. "Aye, it has—five years, maybe, an' another three stone from the looks of ya, Tom. Joshua, meet Thomas St. James, though saint he not be. One time second story man in 'is lighter days, whore's minder, cash carrier, demander...Seen as much time in prison as out, 'aven't ya Tommy?" There was no ill-will in MacLeish's voice and Pitt could discern a trace of a smile on his face.

"You will be knowin' my docket better'n I do, Angus, but I'm straight now an 'ave been these three years. What brings you 'ere?"

"Mr. Pitt, 'ere, is tinkin' 'e 'as some business with ya. I'm just along for ta cab ride, so to speak."

St. James turned slightly in Pitt's direction, and though there was a smile on his face, it was as if the reason for the smile had passed away, and what lingered had a hint of malice in it. He didn't speak directly to Pitt. "And what business would the lad be havin' with me?"

Pitt stepped forward to the edge of the desk. "I want to buy back the two Courvoisier kegs Kevin Wallace sold you last night."

"Who might Kevin Wallace be?"

Pitt ignored the question. "I could simply take them because they're stolen property, but I'll give you what you paid for them."

"Take 'em!" St. James started to rise but stopped midway as MacLeish came around the side of the desk.

"Tommy, me lad, tis not a police matter yet but it could bloody well come tae that if ya decide ta play rough. Pitt made ya an offer, din't he? More'n I would do. Take 'im up on it." He looked from Pitt to St. James. "Besides, I tink ta lad ud give ya a sound thrashing."

St. James sat down. "Give him eight pounds for both, dint I? 'E put them in yon cupboard in the corner."

Pitt walked to the cupboard, opened it and sitting just inside the door were the two kegs, one on top of the other. He picked up one and handed it to MacLeish, then picked up the other, set it on St. James' desk and took eight pounds from his wallet. As he handed the money to St. James, he asked, "Do you know what is in these kegs?"

"Why, brandy, o'course."

"You obviously didn't lift them."

"No, Wallace put 'em in the cupboard."

"It's tobacco—a special blend of tobacco."

"Tobac! Tobac!" Which is all St. James was sputtering and muttering as Pitt and MacLeish walked out the door.

They hailed a four-wheeler, told the cabbie to take them to Bradley's and placed the tobacco between them on the floor of the cab. As if on que, they both pulled their pipes from their pockets and lit up. MacLeish took several puffs, tamped his pipe with his index finger, and said, "Weel, laddie, ya certainly called tha' one right. I suspect Tommy won't be sayin' word to a soul. Embarrassed, he will be. 'Ow might ya wanta 'andle Kevin Wallace?"

"I've been thinking about that, Mac. He's done at Bradley's for sure, but other than a bit of your time and mine, and scaring the bejesus out of Mick, I'm thinking there's no real harm done. No doubt Mick could press charges and the lad would spend Christmas in Gael but what's the purpose? I think scaring the hell out of him should be sufficient."

MacLeish smiled. "Aye, and he's from Scotland, then…"

Pitt smiled back. "Yes…he's from Scotland."

"Now if I were tae suggest, darbys in hand, mind ya, that 'e return tae the confines o' hearth an' 'ome for Christmas, or mayhap a wee bit longer…"

"I think that's a sparkling idea, Mac."

The ride to Bradley's was but a few pleasant minutes of conversation, though the air had chilled noticeably and a light snow had begun to fall. When they arrived, Pitt had the cabbie stop short of the shop and out of sight, where they unloaded the kegs of tobacco. MacLeish stood watch while Pitt went in. Mick was alone and looked up as he came through the door.

"Have you had any luck, then?"

"Are you alone, Mick?"

"Basil's in back and Kevin is due in a few minutes."

"I'll be right back."

A few seconds later, he reentered the shop followed by a snow dusted MacLeish, each carrying a keg of tobacco. They set them on the floor in plain sight at the end of the main counter. Mick, unlit pipe in one hand and match in the other, obviously astonished, looked from kegs to MacLeish and Pitt several times before he spoke.

"Where…? How…?"

"I'll explain all in a few minutes," said Pitt, smiling. "Right now, and before Kevin comes in, I'd like to take another look at the GBD that has disappeared from the display case. I expect we'll get an interesting response when Kevin spots the kegs sitting on the floor."

"Then it was him that took—"

"The pipe, Mick! And hand another to Inspector MacLeish. We'll be perspective customers when he comes through the door." Looking at the expression on Mick's face, Pitt added, "And don't give us away. In fact, don't say anything. I think the Inspector and I can handle this nicely."

No more than a moment later, Kevin Wallace strode in through the door, paused to shake the snow off his umbrella, and smiled at a stone faced Mick as he said, "Good morning to all." It was then he noticed the kegs on the floor at the end of the counter and froze in his tracks, startled and mouth open.

Mick started around the end of the counter. "You thieving bastard!"

Kevin turned to run out the door but was blocked by a grinning MacLeish, pipe in one hand and darbys in the other. "You'll nowt be goin' anywhere, me lad."

Pitt moved between Mick and Kevin and put his hand on the tobacconist's shoulder. "I think we can leave these two, Mick. Let's step to the back room for a few minutes."

Pitt steered Mick to the rear of the shop and walked to the back door. "Before we talk of what to do with Kevin, let me show you how he stole the tobacco, and why." At the door, he lifted the L shaped bar from the iron rings and pointed to a couple of fine scratches right at the bend in the bar. "When Kevin set the lock on the back door last evening, he wrapped a length of fine wire, piano wire probably, around the bend in the bar and ran both ends out through the small crack at the top corner of the door. Look closely and you can see some fine lines in the paint that were made when the wire was pulled from the outside. He came round late, but still well before eleven o'clock because he wanted to make it to the Black Dog tavern before closing. You see, Kevin thought he was stealing expensive cognac, not tobacco, though I dare say the lighter weight of the kegs should have given him pause. But then, he may have simply thought they weren't quite full.

"He pulled both ends of the wire from the outside, raising the bar, and unlocking the door. He then moved the kegs outside, setting them on the skid a few feet away, then positioned the bar in the top ring of the door and closed it. At that point, he loosed one end of the wire and gently pulled on the other, allowing the weight of the bar to drop it into place through the remaining rings. Whether he used a handcart or carried the kegs, I cannot be certain, but from the track in the dirt at the edge of the cobbles, I suspect he used a cart. In any case, he took them to the Black Dog and sold them to the proprietor as Courvoisier for eight pounds. Accompanied by MacLeish, who lent an official air to the task, I simply went to the Black Dog and bought them back."

"Then I owe you eight pounds in addition to my gratitude," said Mick, turning to move to the front of the shop. "I'll take it out of that wee bastard's hide!"

Pitt stopped him with a hand on his shoulder. "Don't let your Irish get the best of you, my friend. I think MacLeish will see to any funds Kevin may have, and he may still have it all. You could press charges of course, but this incident may simply be one best ignored. Charges would require explanations to Mr. Fairbanks that you might want to avoid, and I'm sure MacLeish can convince Kevin that Scotland, in spite of the weather, has a much healthier climate this time of year than does London. What say you?"

Mick thought for a moment, then turned to Pitt. "What you say is the prudent course, I'm sure, but I'd still like to thrash the bastard for all the trouble…"

"Well, he'll be leaving London under a cloud and I suspect he'll not be showing his face around here again." Pitt laughed as a thought came to him. "I doubt he'll be asking you for a referral, either."

Mick grinned. "It would seem unlikely."

They returned to the front of the shop where MacLeish had walked Kevin to a corner and had hold of his coat. "Seems ta lad 'as six pounds he'd like to give you, Mr. Pitt." He looked at Mick. "Will there be charges filed, then?"

Mick, who had already made up his mind not to file charges, took his time answering, and Kevin, a terrified look on his face, cast his eyes down to the shop floor. To Inspector MacLeish, Mick asked, "How much time do you think this thief would get for a robbery of this sort?"

"A year ta Newgate, maybe, or a reformatory if 'e's lucky."

Kevin Wallace appeared to be near tears as he looked up. "Ach, Jasus…"

Mick looked from the inspector to Kevin. "Well, it would serve him right, but I'll abide by whatever the inspector suggests."

MacLeish handed Pitt the money and still holding Kevin tightly by the arm, turned him toward the door. "Alright, lad, you an' me will be takin' a little walk."

As they went out the door, Pitt turned to Mick. "I'll take a look at the GBD Billiard again, Mick."

"My God, Mr. Pitt, take your pick of any pipe in the shop! There's a more expensive line in the front case there…"

"No, I think this GBD will do nicely. Thick shank and not too long. Should be a fine smoke. Ah…here's the good inspector back, and without his charge. Get away from you then, did he, Mac?"

With a grin, and a gleam in his eye, MacLeish said, "Aye, in a manner of speakin'. I suggested Edinburgh might be a safer place for 'im for a while an' if 'e hurried, 'e might be able to get a train yet this mornin'. Gone in a flash, 'e were."

Mick had moved one of the Courvoisier tobacco kegs to a side shelf and was removing the collar at one end. "You gentlemen will both be having a couple of ounces of fine tobac to take with you before you leave the shop. Inspector, would you be interested in taking a look at a pipe? Take your pick of any in the front case at no charge. There's no cost to you this day, that's for certain."

MacLeish smiled. "Weel, now tha' you mention it, tha' half bent right tae front would carry nice in me pocket."

Mick went round the counter, lifted out the pipe, handed it to the inspector, then finished wrapping a couple of ounces of tobacco for each man in thick, waxed paper. As he did, Pitt went over to the keg and put his face over the open end. "That's a rich blend alright, and with mild almond and caramel overtones picked up from the brandy and wood, I'd venture. It should sell out, Mick."

"Thanks to you gentlemen, we have it to sell. If there's some other way I can show my appreciation…"

"No, no," said Pitt, filling the bowl of his new pipe from the keg, "a pipe and tobacco is more than enough, wouldn't you say, Mac?"

"Aye, more'n I expected when I left ta Yard this mornin'."

It had stopped snowing and both men stopped outside the shop to light their pipes while looking up and down the street for a hansom.

Pitt took several short puffs, then tamped the tobacco down and relit. "Did you leave him train fare, then?"

"Aye, 'e 'ad all eight pounds on 'im. I gave you six and 'eld back two for 'is trip. Didn't think Mick would be pressin' charges."

"So I financed his journey back home, did I?"

"Aye, ya might be sayin' that." MacLeish was smiling over the bowl of his new pipe while putting another match to it. "Whilst you were in back explainin' to Mick 'ow 'e done it, 'e were explainin' to me up front. Shrewd piece o' work, that."

"That it was, Mac, that it was. Well, let's just be glad he's no longer in London or I think you'd be meeting him again."

"Aye, and no pipe and tobac for my efforts either…"

END

THE AMESBURY AFFAIR

Still in bed, he heard the tap at the door, the turn of the lock and familiar "Seven o'clock, Mr. Pitt," as Mrs. Keating bustled into the flat and put the tea tray on his desk in the front room he used as an office.

"Thank you, Mrs. Keating."

"Fog this morning."

"I thought so." He didn't have to be told. The bedroom window was slightly ajar and wisps of thick yellow fog entered the room and then slipped back out as if the walls were breathing. It was smog, actually, a November smog from thousands of coal fires in London. He rose, donning a thick quilted robe as he did, and walked to the window. The gaslight on the corner just a few yards away was barely visible. He heard his landlady close the door as he walked to the front of his flat. Mrs. Keating was a delightful widow in her fifties; a woman of even temperament and best of all, a good cook.

He finished his toilet, sat down at his desk, removed the tea cozy and poured tea into a large mug. While it cooled, he filled a pipe, lit it, tamped and lit it again, enjoying the aroma and flavor of his first bowl of the day. It was an old bent Peterson pipe; one he'd bought during a layover in Dublin during the two years he'd worked on the Laura, a packet freighter out of Southampton. The ship carried mostly wool and dry goods and made regular voyages to Cork, Dublin, Belfast, Glasgow and back to Southampton. He'd held the job longer than any other, partly because he enjoyed the ever-changing sea and partly because he earned enough to bank a few pounds each payday. But there was no challenge to the job and he eventually tired of it. He earned a reputation as a hard worker and problem solver with an analytical mind, and often found solutions to problems when others could not. It was one such instance when he managed to discover why the ship's log had disappeared, that the Captain suggested he'd do well as a detective. And when he determined he'd saved enough to keep himself afloat financially for at least six months, he quit the Laura and settled in London. He'd found rooms near Regent's Park, at 22C Baker Street that served as office, sitting room and bedroom, and opened up shop as a private inquiry agent. That had been almost a year past, and more than a dozen cases that had enhanced his reputation as well as his bank account. His financial solvency could be seen in the growing number of pipes that sat in racks on his desk and bookshelf, in addition to several large glass containers of tobacco.

He had finished his scone and was taking a sip of tea when there was a knock at the door. Thinking it was Mrs. Keating coming back for the tea tray, he said, "Come in, I'm just finished."

The door opened and a short, stout man wearing an ulster and bowler hat stepped into the room. His dark beard was flecked with grey and a pair of reading glasses perched on the end of his nose. Belying his bulk, he moved lightly to the chair in front of the desk, removed his bowler, and pulled a pipe from his pocket.

"Would you be havin' a spot of tea left for an old copper on a cold, foggy morning, then?"

Pitt smiled. "I suppose you'd like a bowl of tobacco with it?"

"Aye, tha' would be nice."

Pitt slid a jar of tobacco toward his visitor and then poured a cup of tea. "So what brings Inspector MacLeish out so early on a dreary morning?"

"Mr. Arthur Amesbury, or tae be more exact, seein' that 'e's dead, Mrs. Arthur Amesbury. Seems as you did 'er a good turn a while back and she could use another. If I'm not mistaken, she'll be accused of murderin' 'er husband afore the day is out."

Pitt remembered her well. Several months before, he'd been instrumental in recovering some jewelry her husband had sold to support his drinking, gambling, and weekly visits to some of the better-known high class brothels. It had cost her the sale price but she was willing to pay. They'd belonged to her mother.

"How'd he die?"

"Poison…strychnine—at least that's what our Dr. Morgan thinks. 'E's conducting the autopsy an' we'll be knowin' for certain sometime this afternoon. Mrs. Amesbury is resting tae home, under police observation, of course."

"And Mrs. Amesbury asked for me?"

"Aye, tha' she did. One of the few things she 'as said. A constable let slip we'd be treating this as a suspicious death and a few minutes later she says tae me, 'Get me Joshua Pitt,' so 'ere I am." He tamped and relit his pipe. "Not that I normally run errands for the accused, so tae speak, but our paths 'ave crossed several times in a friendly way an' favors have a way of bein' paid back."

Pitt leaned back in his chair and took several puffs on his pipe, thinking. "If it was poison, what leads you to believe it was Mrs. Amesbury?"

"Well now…we both know tha' poisonin' is never an impulsive crime. The poisoner has to have some kind of relationship with the person they're going to kill, and it's usually one of trust, like a family member. Ta be honest, knowing Mr. Amesbury as I did, I'm surprised she didn't poison 'im a long time ago. A right rotten bastard 'e was, an' tha' might mitigate in her favor, but I'm no the judge."

The Inspector was right about poisoning, thought Pitt. Either someone close or someone trusted, or both. Dr. Thomas Neill Cream who poisoned at least a dozen women and one man, came readily to mind.

"So, how did it happen, Angus?"

"Well, they 'ad dinner, dint they, and the deceased 'ad changed clothes and was getting ready tae leave the house. One of his weekly jaunts tae a West End whore, I expect. According tae their butler, 'e made it tae front hallway before keeling over in what appeared tae be great pain. They sent for a doctor of course, but it were too late. 'E was dead by the time ta doctor arrived. The doctor sent for police. We collected what remaining food was left over from dinner but since they were served and both ate the same ting, we'll 'ave little luck there, I'm tinkin'. Amesbury drank most of a bottle of French white with dinner but the bottle is nowhere to be found and the wine glass had been washed. Suspicious…"

"Are you returning to Amesbury Manor?"

"No till later. I'm tae go back tae me office when I leave here."

The Inspector stood, picked up his bowler, and shook hands with Pitt. "Nice tobacco. What is it?"

"Arcadia. Take some for your pouch if you like."

"No, I'll be stickin' with me shag. I'm used tae it."

"If I learn anything, Angus, I'll share it."

"T'would be appreciated."

The fog was lifting as Pitt hailed a Hansom and settled back for the half hour trip to Amesbury Manor. Lucy Amesbury didn't strike him as a poisoner. More the long suffering wife, though she'd shown traces of deep anger when he reported that her jewelry had been stolen and sold by her husband. Pitt hinted at the reasons, but her expression told him she already knew. In fact, she had said, "There's no need for subtlety, Mr. Pitt. I know my husband's habits." He did learn they had separate bedrooms and suspected there'd been no physical contact between them for a long time, perhaps several years.

The Manor was an imposing stone structure of a dozen rooms or more with a tree lined driveway leading up to the entrance. Pitt told the cabby to wait, walked to the front door and gave the bell ringer a twist. It was answered by the butler. Though he knew Hastings from previous visits, he handed him his card.

"Joshua Pitt to see Mrs. Amesbury."

"Right this way sir. She's expecting you."

Pitt followed him up the stairs and along a hallway to a room at the end. Hastings tapped and then opened the door. "Mr. Pitt, ma'am."

It was a large, combined bedroom-sitting room decorated in pastels of pink and blue. Mrs. Amesbury, in a dressing gown, was on a settee near the window. She was an attractive woman of about thirty with chestnut hair, hazel eyes, and a fine figure not well hidden by the bulk of the gown.

"Please sit down, Mr. Pitt. Hastings, ask Mattie to bring us some tea." As she turned toward Pitt, sunlight streaming through the window highlighting her hair, showing touches of auburn he hadn't seen before. He also noticed a fading bruise on her right cheek.

"Since you're here, Mr. Pitt, I assume Inspector MacLeish has talked with you. I also assume he told you they suspect me of poisoning my husband."

"Did you?"

"No…but I daresay they may not believe me. Though not widely known, my husband's treatment of me and his uncivil habits were obvious to many, including, I suspect, Inspector MacLeish."

"He probably knows more of the details than you do, ma'am.

"No doubt. And no doubt those details, as you call them, will play an important role in his decision to arrest me or not."

"MacLeish is a cautious man. Given your position in the community, I doubt he'll make any move against you before he has substantial proof."

"God knows I wished my husband dead or gone on many occasions, but I didn't kill him, Mr. Pitt." She paused, and then with a flash of temper looked up at him. "It's a crime against women, Mr. Pitt, that English law binds wives to men such as my husband!"

Though he agreed, Pitt ignored the opening and kept to the subject. "Tell me then, of last evening, with as much detail as you remember."

"Arthur came home about five o'clock. I was in the study reviewing the house ledgers and making out some checks. He'd been drinking, as usual, and when he saw the checks he asked me to make out one to cash for fifty pounds. I refused. For a moment, I thought he was going to leave, but he then took a quick step forward and slapped me with the back of his hand. He said if I didn't give him the money, he'd fix my face so I'd be ashamed to leave the house for a month. Not long ago, I threatened to cut off any money for his frolics but when he was drinking…" She shrugged her shoulders. "I made out a check and he stormed out. Dinner was at seven and he seemed in a good mood, though I suspect it was because he planned an evening frolic somewhere. He left the table slightly before eight, saying he was going to his room, and I went to the library for a small brandy and coffee.

"About twenty minutes later, I heard a sound on the stairs as though someone had fallen, or at least stumbled a couple of steps and caught themselves. No more than a few seconds later, I heard a horrible scream and rushed into the hallway. Arthur was near the front door, writhing on the floor in terrible pain. He was actually frothing at the mouth with his face and body contorted in agony. His eyes were open, staring, but as if he were seeing nothing. Hastings had come out of the dining room and was kneeling next to him. As I knelt down, I told Hastings to send for a doctor and he left. Arthur grabbed my arm, looked at me, and tried to say something but I couldn't make it out. He had another seizure, gripping my arm so that I had to pry his hand loose. I think he was dead then. After a moment, I got to my feet and sat in one of the hallway chairs. I couldn't bear to look at him. His face…twisted in a mask of pain…Hastings returned, asked if he could get me something, and told me the doctor would be here quickly. The doctor arrived within minutes, examined Arthur, told me he was gone and asked Hastings to summon the police. I retired to my room."

Pitt sat staring out the window over her shoulder, mentally reviewing what had been said and considering questions he might ask.

"How is it that you decided to contact me? Inspector MacLeish is a fair and conscientious man who wouldn't bring charges without foundation."

"The Inspector may be fair, as you say, but it would soon be out of his hands. After being questioned, it was Hastings who suggested I call upon you. Please feel free to smoke your pipe if you like, Mr. Pitt. I enjoy the aroma of tobacco.

"Thank you, ma'am, I'll do that. Seems to help me think."

"Please call me Lucy. Given the circumstances, and our previous acquaintance over a related matter, formalities seem inappropriate."

"Alright, Lucy…The doctor that came last night—was he your regular physician?"

"He's mine. Dr. Cartwright was Arthur's too until several months ago when he began visiting a doctor in the city."

"You said he got here within minutes…"

"He lives just four houses away. It's just a couple minutes walk."

"I'd like to speak with him."

"Of course. I'll write a note asking him to answer any questions you have."

"Though it seems unlikely, is there any possibility your husband committed suicide? Had he been in ill health—mentally or physically?"

She stared at him for a moment. "I hardly know how to answer. He seemed fit enough, though if he had any physical problems he wouldn't have confided in me. We rarely had any conversation. As to mental…I don't know…He drank daily, often all day, and may have been using other substances as well. Suicide never occurred to me. He was on his way out for the night."

"When you say out for the night, do you mean he'd be back late or not till the next day sometime."

"If he had money, not till the next day, or maybe two days. And he had fifty pounds…"

While they were talking, tea had arrived. Pitt relit his pipe, taking several puffs as Lucy poured.

"That's a nice aroma. What tobacco is it?"

"Arcadia." Pitt smiled. "You're the second person to ask that today."

"Who was the first?"

"Inspector MacLeish."

"I expect he'll be back to arrest me…"

"He'll be back, certainly, but I don't think he'll arrest you. He thinks he has motive but lacks any hard evidence tying you directly to your husband's death. As I said, he's a cautious man. I do expect he'll leave a PC on duty here and ask you not to leave for the time being."

"I didn't kill my husband, Mr. Pitt," she said emphatically, "and in any case, have no plans to go anywhere."

"Since we're on a first name basis, you can call me Joshua, or simply Pitt, as many of my friends do. Before I leave to see Dr. Cartwright, I'd like to look at your husband's bedroom."

"Of course, Pitt, we can do that now."

"And I'd also like a few moments with your house staff if you don't mind."

"Certainly."

Arthur Amesbury's bedroom was located at the opposite end of the hallway, which surprised him. While it was not unusual for a wealthy husband and wife to have separate bedrooms, they were usually adjoining. Pitt declined to comment on this but as they entered the room, Lucy said, "His bedroom was next to mine until two years ago when I told him coming in after midnight several nights a week, and creating a disturbance, was waking me and unacceptable. He moved the following week and we converted the small room next to this one to a WC. I haven't been disturbed at night since."

Without her saying so, Pitt took this to mean conjugal visits ceased at the same time, if not before. The bedroom was neat and clean, as it would be with servants in the house and he saw nothing out of the ordinary. He opened the drawers of a small chest but there were only some underclothes, socks, and a small shaving kit with razor, cologne, and a bar of soap wrapped in a washcloth.

The adjoining WC was more interesting. Aside from bathtub and toilet, there was a linen cabinet, the top two shelves stocked with a variety of potions and pills, perhaps a dozen in all. Some he was familiar with and some not. Several he recognized, were touted as aphrodisiacs. He took a pencil and small notebook from his jacket pocket.

"I'll take a few minutes and make a list of these."

"While you're doing that, I'll gather the staff in the kitchen. When you're ready, you can see them there. I'll be in my room if you need see me before you leave."

"I don't think that will be necessary but I expect to return tomorrow morning."

"I may not be here if Inspector MacLeish has his way."

"He doesn't have enough evidence for a warrant, or at least he didn't this morning and I expect he has little more now. I do expect him to be here this afternoon with additional questions, however. Answer truthfully, but don't volunteer information."

Pitt finished in Amesbury's bedroom and went to the kitchen. There were four members to the household staff: the butler Hastings, a housemaid, scullery maid, and cook. They could add little to what he already knew. Both Mr. and Mrs. Amesbury were served equally from the food that had been prepared. Mrs. Amesbury had drunk tea while Mr. Amesbury had wine. There was nothing unusual in that—Mrs. Amesbury rarely drank any alcoholic beverage. The dinnerware had been washed as usual, at the end of the meal, and that included water and wine glasses. Pit noticed that none of the staff seemed particularly depressed at the death of Amesbury, though he hardly found it surprising given Amesbury's reputation as a churlish lout. He thanked them for their time and made his way to the front of the manor, preparing to leave. As he stopped in the doorway to light his pipe, Hastings touched his arm.

"A word, sir?"

"What is it, Hastings?"

"Madam asked me to give you this envelope for Dr. Cartwright. And then, sir, about the wine bottle…There was a bit more than a glass left in the bottle and I poured a small one for myself before taking the bottle to the bin behind the kitchen. I'm not surprised that it's gone though. Tramps come through this area regularly and take any usable leftovers from the bin. They usually come through soon after dinner."

"Did you tell that to Inspector MacLeish?"

"No sir. I suspect Missus Amesbury knows I occasionally help myself to a glass but I didn't want to take a chance on getting the sack if the Mister found out." He paused, the corners of his mouth twitching in a controlled smile. "Though that's no longer an issue now, is it sir?"

"No, it's not. Thank you for telling me, Hastings. I see no need for it to go any further unless it becomes necessary to use that information to protect Mrs. Amesbury."

"I understand, sir."

Pitt had kept the hansom waiting and gave directions to Dr. Cartwright's residence. Since it was only a few houses away, he could have walked, but wanted the hansom with him. He walked to the door, pocketed his pipe, rang the bell and waited. He was about to ring again when the door was opened abruptly dour faced old woman dressed completely in brown. It was hard to judge her age—seventy perhaps—maybe even more. Her hair was completely grey and her face and neck wrinkled like a dried prune. It was as if she had one time weighed considerably more and with age and loss of weight, her skin had nowhere to go but inward in folds and creases.

Looking him over from head to foot, she said, "Doctor doesn't see patients ta home. He'll be ta surgery on the morrow, past mid day," and started to close the door.

Pitt stopped the door with his hand. "I'm not a patient. I'm here to see the doctor about another matter."

"What be the matter, then?"

Seeing no need to hide the reason and assuming most in the neighborhood already knew of the death of Amesbury, he replied, "It's about Mr. Amesbury who was once a patient of the doctors."

"Humph. Good riddance ta that 'un. You a copper?"

"No, a friend of Mrs. Amesbury's. I take it you didn't like her husband."

"Caused her a lot of grief, he did." She motioned him inside and without another word, walked down the long hallway expecting him to follow, which he did. At the end of the hallway was a door marked *Laboratory*. She tapped lightly, then opened the door.

"Gentleman ta see you, Doctor."

The doctor was standing at a lab counter facing away from the door, and writing in a large notebook.

"Show him in, Anna."

The housekeeper pointed Pitt to a desk with a side chair and he walked to it but remained standing. Cartwright was younger than he'd imagined, perhaps early forties, balding but with a large mustache, and easily six feet tall. His dress was a bit eccentric, or so Pitt thought. The doctor was wearing a pale brown tweed coat that bagged at the leather patched elbows and pockets, and a pair of dark brown corduroy knickerbockers. The vision was more that of a country veterinarian than a doctor with a successful city practice. Pitt was still staring at him when he finished writing and turned around.

"And how can I be of service to you, Mr...?"

"Pitt...Joshua Pitt." He handed Lucy's note to the doctor. "At Mrs. Amesbury's request, I'm looking into the matter of her husband's death."

"Hmmm...yes...undoubtedly poison but I doubt it is official yet. If I were to hazard a guess, I'd say strychnine. Rotten way to go at any age but for a man in his late 30's...Still, I doubt he will be missed by anyone except for the whores he kept. Mistreated Lucy terribly, both emotionally and physically. A singularly rotten blighter in the truest sense."

"He harmed her physically?"

"Beat her several times, or so I surmise. Though the last time she came to me was about four months ago. She said she fell, but I told her straight out it was untrue. She began to cry and I told her to confront Arthur that evening before he was too drunk to understand and tell him the next time he raised a hand to her, she'd cut off his funds. She must have done so, because she hasn't been back to see me, or perhaps she's been too embarrassed. She certainly had reason to do away with him, though I doubt even a sympathetic jury would save her from the gallows."

"You think she poisoned him?"

"Logical conclusion, and I expect the same one the police will arrive at."

"I found a collection of patent medicines in Mr. Amesbury's cabinet, three of which I was unfamiliar with. I wrote them down." He handed the list to the doctor.

Cartwright looked it over. "The first is easy enough. *Martin's Elixir*, a hangover remedy, though I daresay the only ingredient of any benefit is the grain alcohol it's fortified with. Probably 50 percent. The other two, I'm unfamiliar with—*Prime* and *Flack's Mixture*. That last one reminds me of something though. Amesbury was last here about three months ago, his second visit in a week. Problems with his masculinity, as he put it. Couldn't perform. Alcohol, of course. It's a wonder after a nights drinking he could even think about a prostitute, let alone…I told him to cut back on his drinking but he'd have none of it. Said something about visiting a doctor in the East End. Flack, as I recall."

"He didn't say where in the East End?"

"No, I'm afraid not."

"How well do you know Mrs. Amesbury?"

"Professionally, of course, though until three years ago there were some social functions we attended together. My wife Sarah knows her better than I. They worked together on several charitable causes. That ended several years ago as well, but they stay in touch." He paused, looking at Pitt. "You don't think she did it, do you?"

"No, doctor, I don't."

"I certainly hope you're right."

"I may need some medical advice, or at least a professional opinion, within a day or so. May I call on you?"

"Of course. Anything I can do to help."

Pitt paused as he climbed into the Hansom. "Have you ever heard of a Doctor Flack, cabbie?"

"Aye, sor, I has. Eastender, I'm thinkin' but I don' know where. I knows a fella who could tell us though, don't I? Is tha' we be headed fur?"

"Yes, it is. How long will it take?"

"'bout 30 minutes. We'll be stoppin' ta see auld Harold. He be knowin' everybody that is anybody in East End…an' some what ain't."

As Pitt sat back in the corner of the cab, he tamped and lit his pipe. Taking short light puffs, as was his wont when thinking through a problem, he began with the assumption that Lucy Amesbury hadn't poisoned her husband, though she certainly had motive and opportunity. Why then, assume she didn't do it? He didn't know. Intuition? He wasn't sure of that feeling either, but Lucy Amesbury committing murder just didn't feel right. Thoughtfully, he moved on. What about the servants? He had the sense that none of them liked Amesbury and might even be relieved he was no longer among the living, but for one of the servants to kill him seemed totally out of place and character. And thinking of being out of place and character, suicide seemed to be the most unlikely cause of death. The man was leaving the house for a night on the town when he collapsed in the hallway. Then again...Well, conjecture and speculation were alright, but it was impossible to put forth a sound case without facts, and at the moment, he only had two: Arthur Amesbury was dead, and he died of poisoning, though poisoning was yet to be confirmed.

His pipe had burned down to a white ash and was out. He tapped the ash into his hand and pitched it out the cab window as they turned into a narrow lane of run-down boarding houses. Coal smoke, dirty streets and open sewers combined with the smell of cooking cabbage to descend on the cab with the pale yellow fog, while rubbish and feces flowed in a stew along the gutters. The hansom drew up in front of a tavern aptly named *Hogs Blood* and the cabbie climbed down to open the door.

"Old Harold be holdin' court in 'ere, gov'nor. 'E's a strange cove wi' a crossed eye an' game leg, but 'e knows all wot goes on 'ere."

More than one head turned in their direction as they entered and made their way toward an alcove at the rear of the room. They stopped in front of an old, grey haired man seated alone at a table. He was staring at a half filled pint of Guinness, watching a fly swimming around the edge of the stout looking for a way out.

"Gent 'ere would buy ya a drink, Harold."

Harold looked at them both at the same time, one eye crossing to take in Pitt. "Aye, tha' be nice." He lifted his glass and drank it down, fly and all. "Sit ye."

The cabbie motioned to the landlord with three fingers up. "Gent 'ere needs some information about Dr. Flack."

The eye crossed to Pitt again. "This be a payin' question?"

"A quid if the information is good...and complete."

"Christ! For a quid I'd tell ya who me dead mum slept wi' last night."

"Just Flack will do." The landlord arrived with the Guinness.

"Aye. Well...Flack be new to the East End. New to England too, seein 'e's from Australia. Calls hisself doctor but I doubts it. Sells mostly potions and such to any cove what can't keep his cod up…or get it up. I hear tell he sells syrup wi' cocaine as well. Some women like it…mostly whores."

"Anyone ever get sick taking his medicine?"

"Not tha' I heerd of, but folks here die all the time o' one thing t'other. Gin mostly, I 'spect. Flack's got rooms an' surgery on Philpot at Ashfield Street, Stepney."

Pitt left money on the table for drinks and Harold and motioned the cabbie to go. Tossing down the rest of his stout, then wiping his mouth with the back of his hand, the cabbie stood and moved to the door.

"Flack's then, is it?"

"Flack's."

The ride was a short one, no more than a few minutes, but enough time for Pitt to consider how he was going to approach the doctor. He'd originally thought straight forward—that he was investigating the circumstances of Amesbury's death but now thought better of it. It was unlikely that Amesbury's death had been widely reported as yet, and Pitt was now a man in need of a tonic.

The door of Flack's surgery was opened by a young lad of perhaps fifteen dressed in clean white shirt and dark trousers. He was blonde and fair, almost pretty.

"Can I help you sir?"

"Is the doctor in?"

"Aye sir, he is. Can I 'ave your name?"

"Mr. Pitt."

The lad disappeared through a door at the end of the anti-room and Pitt took a seat in one of four chairs along the wall. From the looks of it, the room had recently been painted a pale green and there was carpet on the floor, worn but swept clean. He didn't have long to wait. The door opened and a short, medium built man of about 40 came into the room. He was five foot six or seven, clean-shaven, with sandy colored hair and dark complexion. He stepped forward to shake hands and Pitt stood up.

"Mr. Pitt?"

"Yes. And you're Dr. Flack?"

"Correct, sir. Would you step into my consulting room, please?" He motioned to the open doorway.

The consulting room was the same color of green but the carpet was better. The doctor slid behind his desk and motioned to a side chair.

"What seems to be the problem, Mr. Pitt?"

"Well, it's a bit embarrassing, doctor, but my relationships with the ladies have taken a turn for the worse lately. I'm unable to perform as I used to."

Flack smiled. "How old are you?"

"Twenty-eight"

"That's a bit young to have such a problem."

"That's what disturbs me, doctor."

"Well, you look healthy enough. What are your drinking habits?"

"No more than the next man, I suppose. Though on occasion…"

"I see…Are those the time when you have a problem?"

"That did happen once or twice, but the last couple of times I've had little to drink, maybe two or three pints."

"How did you come to hear of me?"

"About a week ago, I was having a drink with Arthur Amesbury and when he pointed out a fair lass, I jokingly made a comment I'd do something about her if I could. He said if I was having a problem I should see Dr. Flack. That you had some tonics that might help me. After another failed attempt last night, I decided to look you up."

"Did Mr. Amesbury happen to mention which tonics?"

"One of them had your name and the other was called "Original" or "Finest" or something like that."

"That would be *Flack's Mixture* and *Prime*. I've had some success with those but must caution you not to expect too much. I can give you both preparations but if your problem continues beyond several weeks, I suggest you see a specialist that deals in the physical aspects of dysfunction."

Flack left the room for a few moments and returned with two small bottles similar to what Pitt had seen at Amesbury's. "The directions and dosage are on the labels. You shouldn't exceed the dosage indicated. It may cause digestive problems if you do."

"Thank you, doctor. If they don't have the expected result, I'll see a specialist as you suggest." Pitt paid the fee and returned to the Hansom, telling the cabbie to take him to his rooms on Baker Street.

Mrs. Keating was sweeping the steps in front of her home when the hansom came to a halt at the kerb. Pitt paid the driver and made arrangements to be picked up at eight o'clock the following morning.

"Have you supped yet, Mr. Pitt?"

"No, I haven't and I'm starved."

"I'll be bringing some fresh ham and potatoes up to you in a few minutes then. Would you like tea or beer?"

"A half pitcher of beer sounds wonderful, thank you."

Pitt walked upstairs to his rooms, and stopping at his desk, placed the two bottles Doctor Flack had prepared for him next to his pipe rack. He removed his coat and scarf, and hung them on the coat tree behind the desk before settling into the chair and selecting a pipe. He was still gently puffing away and staring at the bottles when Mrs. Keating tapped on the door and entered carrying a tray.

"That policeman were here again while you were out. He left a note for you." They were all "policemen" to Mrs. Keating, regardless of rank. She handed Pitt a folded piece of paper. He thanked her, unfolded the note and set it beside the tray to read as he ate.

> *Pitt—As we suspected, it were strychnine wot did in Amesbury. We've nowt enough against the missus to charge her but I will question her closely late this day. All is suggestive of her having a hand in it—at least my instincts as a copper tell me so. My questioning of the servants and several friends of the family, supports what I knew of him—that he were a course and cruel bastard wot treated her badly. She had both motive and ample opportunity. As yet we find no direct link to her and it may be left to a court of inquiry to determine if charges are laid. Given the lady's standing in the community and her family's reputation, a finding that would put her in the dock is unlikely at this time. If your investigations turn up any useful information, the sharing of it would be greatly appreciated.*
> *MacLeish*

Pitt sat the note aside, finished his meal, and then took it up again after relighting his pipe. It was undeniable that Lucy Amesbury had motive. He'd read that in her face when she talked of her husband. Opportunity was another matter. She had none at dinner and had no contact with her husband between the meal and when he was leaving for the evening. Yet he died before he could get out of the house. A measure of strychnine large enough to fell the man as it did, could not have been ingested at dinner, but only a short time before—perhaps minutes. To Pitt, that meant only one thing: that Amesbury had poisoned himself. Unintentionally or accidentally, perhaps, but nonetheless, self-administered. MacLeish's instincts were not to be ignored, however. Plodder that he was, in his almost thirty years on the force he had built sound reputation based on a string of successes. Well...perhaps he'd learn more in the morning. He planned to stop at the Amesbury estate, pick up the medicines from Amesbury's WC and take them to Doctor Cartwright with the samples he'd obtained earlier from Flack. Maybe analysis would tell him something.

He picked up his dinner tray and carried it downstairs to Mrs. Keating. She was pouring a large mug of tea as he walked into her kitchen.

"That was delicious, Mrs. Keating, just delicious."

"You liked it then. That's fine. I was going to be bringing you some tea but you can save me a trip. I did the stairs today and my knees are bothering me."

"Why don't you bring someone in to do the stairs? It certainly wouldn't cost much and I'd be glad to pay for it."

"That's kind of you, Mr. Pitt, and you've offered before, but as long as I can do it myself, I will."

"Well, thank you again for dinner. Oh, could you check to see that I'm awake about 6:30 tomorrow? I have a long day planned."

"I'll do that, then. Sleep fair, Mr. Pitt."

"Good night, now."

Tea in hand, he climbed the stairs to his rooms and placed it on his desk before selecting another pipe from his rack. He filled and lit it, then sat at his desk thinking while he sipped tea and smoked. He mentally reviewed the day and reread MacLeish's note, but finding that he wasn't getting anywhere, decided on bed. He suspected it would be a long day tomorrow.

He was sitting on the edge of the bed when the draft of Mrs. Keating opening his front door pulled the smell of rain and fog in through the partially open window.

"Six-thirty, Mr. Pitt."

"Thank you, Mrs. Keating."

"Raining steady...and there's a chill in the air."

"Thank you again."

He slipped on his heavy cotton robe, walked to the front room, and poured tea into a large mug. While it cooled, he filled a pipe, lit it, and sat at his desk. The aroma of pipe tobacco and hot Assam tea filled the room. He'd acquired a taste for the strong, black Indian tea somewhere along the way, and when he mentioned it to Mrs. Keating, she promptly laid in a supply, serving him a full pot with fresh scones each morning.

He finished breakfast, completed his toilet, and dressed for the day. Before leaving, he put two pipes and a pouch of tobacco in his ulster pocket. Should last the day, he thought, but if not, he was due to stop by his tobacconists anyway. His hansom was waiting in front as he walked out the door.

"Mornin' Gov. Where we be off to today?"

"The Amesbury estate first."

"Right ya are, Gov."

The cabbie flicked his whip to the side of the horse's head and they moved off as Pitt was settled back into the seat. He lit a pipe and stared out the window, noticing a few flakes of snow falling with the rain. It was not bitterly cold, but cold nonetheless, and his breath mixed with smoke from his pipe before slipping out the window. As much as he wanted to believe Lucy Amesbury had nothing to do with poisoning her husband, the reality was that every intentional poisoning he knew of had been committed by a family member or someone close to the poisoned party. And that, he was sure, was what MacLeish believed. There was the one other possibility though, and he hoped to follow up on it this morning.

As he walked up the steps to the Amesbury manor house, the door opened and Hastings stepped to the side allowing him to enter.

"Good morning, Hastings. Is Mrs. Amesbury in?"

"She is sir, and is expecting you. We're also expecting Inspector MacLeish."

Before shedding his ulster, he removed a pipe and his tobacco pouch, then followed down the hallway to the library where Hastings opened one of the double doors. "Mr. Pitt to see you, ma'am."

"Good morning, Pitt. Hastings, please ask Mattie to bring tea."

Lucy Amesbury was standing to the side of the window with the sunlight playing off her chestnut hair and pale yellow dress. He'd expected to see her dressed in black. He was surprised and his face must have shown it.

"Please sit down, Pitt, and light your pipe if you like." He took a wingback chair near the desk and proceeded to fill his pipe, while she took a seat on a couch a few feet away. "Though I'm officially in mourning, I don't have to abide by the social rule in my own home—not yet anyway. I'll wear black when appropriate." She was smiling. "Does that answer your question?"

"It does. Was I that transparent?"

"I'm afraid so... Or at least I thought so. Have you learned anything since yesterday morning?"

"A little. At least I have a theory but it's only that for now. I'd like your permission to take some of the medicines from your husband's cabinet."

She looked surprised. "Whatever for?"

"I'd like to have them analyzed. It's possible there was something in them that may have caused his death." He put a match to his pipe and took several puffs.

"Now, how could that be? I haven't looked, but I can't imagine anything but headache powders and maybe something for stomach upset, which he seemed to have more often lately. I assumed it was the heavy drinking."

Pitt tamped his pipe and set it on the table. "The heavy drinking may be the root cause of his death."

Again, she looked surprised. "How could…? Do you mean the alcohol combined with a stomach powder could have killed him?"

"Something like that. I'm not sure at this point and before I suggest something along those lines to you or Inspector MacLeish, I want to have some of the medications tested."

"Well then, certainly, take whatever ones you need. I just can't imagine how…"

"As I said, I don't know, but we do know that different people react differently to medications. It's possible he may have had a physical reaction to one of them but if that's the case, we may never know. I'm not sure a medical examination could identify a harmful reaction after the person dies." Pitt wanted to hold off telling Lucy what he suspected for two reasons. First, because he wasn't sure he was on the right track, and second of course, was propriety. Open discussion of sexual matters wasn't considered appropriate in some social circles, though he felt confident he could express himself in acceptable terms to Lucy without going into explicit details if it came to that.

Mattie had come in while they were talking and placed the tea tray on a small table in front of Lucy and then stepped back a pace.

"That will be all for now, Mattie. Thank you."

Pitt watched her walk toward the door, where she paused for a few seconds to look back at them before leaving the room. He felt that had he been alone, she might have had something to say to him. He made a mental note to follow up on it later.

"Are you saying it could have been an accident, Pitt?"

"I'm saying it's possible, though I don't think MacLeish has considered it. But then, I haven't had any word from him since yesterday. He did leave me a note saying that a medical examination determined strychnine was present in your husband's body. I'm assuming he will view that as the direct cause, though I'm not so sure."

Lucy sat quietly for a few minutes sipping her tea. "You're an unusual man, Mr. Pitt, in many respects, but in detecting, I think you're a rare breed. You seem to not accept anything that would seem obvious to others, but instead, dig under the surface for answers."

"Thank you for the compliment, but what I sometimes find is not always to the satisfaction of those who send me looking."

She smiled slightly. "I suspect not, Pitt…I suspect not. Inspector MacLeish is due any time and I think I will receive him in my sitting room. I feel I have an advantage there and with the Inspector, I think I need it. Feel free to take what ever you need from my husband's room." She rose and gathered her skirts around her as she turned toward he door.

Pitt stood and pocketed his pipe. "I may or may not be back later today but in any case will be here tomorrow morning to bring you up to date on anything new."

"Thank you, Pitt. I trust you will find the truth of this matter."

He searched Amesbury's room again, more thoroughly this time, but found nothing out of the ordinary and simply gathered the articles he needed from the WC before walking downstairs to the kitchen. The cook's name was Mary Waite, and unlike most cooks who seem to grow in volume the longer they cook, she was a slender, spare woman of about fifty with salt and pepper hair tied in a bun. She was stacking freshly made crumpets on a tray.

"Would you be havin' a cuppa, sir?"

"That would be nice, thank you. Will you join me?"

"I believe I will, sir. Been busy since six this morning, haven't I?" She poured two cups of tea from a large covered pot, set cream and sugar on the table, and took a seat across from Pitt.

"Have you been with the Amesbury's long, Mary?"

"Thirty-one years last June. I were a young scullery maid then, an' the mistress, she were a just a babe." Her face softened and a hint of a smile appeared. "Tha' were a fine time then. Her mother and father were grand folk. Treated us good, they did, almost like family. Then there were tha' terrible accident on the train from Edinburgh, an' they were gone. The mistress, she were twenty-two at the time."

"Mrs. Amesbury's mother and father were killed in a train accident?"

"Aye sir, they were, an' a shame it were later on too."

"How's that, Mary?"

"I don' be wantin' ta say none bad about the dead but I don't think Mr. Baldwin would have permitted his daughter's marriage ta Mr. Amesbury. Fathers have a way of knowin' or findin' out things that young ladies can't."

"And what would he have found out?"

"'Tis not my place to say, sir."

"Oh surely it is, Mary. Mr. Amesbury's gone now and Mrs. Amesbury could be in deep trouble. You must know the police suspect her of being involved with his death. I can assure you that anything you say to me will not be repeated unless it becomes necessary to protect Mrs. Amesbury."

She got up from the table, lifted the teapot, and refilled their cups before sitting again. She was silent for a moment and Pitt let her think while he took his pipe from his pocket, tamped, and then lit it.

"I like the smell of a pipe," she said. "Mr. Baldwin smoked a pipe but there's been no pipe smoke in this house since." She paused, sipped her tea, and smiled. "That is till you came…Mr. Amesbury ill-treated my mistress, he did. More than once she was in this kitchen for an hour with me puttin' cold compresses on her face where the devil had struck her. And he had women…"

"He had women here?"

"Not here, but there's always the whispers, idn't there? 'cept…"

"Except who, Mary?"

"'Cept Mattie. He tried it with Mattie, didn't he? Right in his room just down the hall from my mistress. But he was drunk…"

"He was drunk and couldn't perform. Is that it, Mary?"

"Aye, he was drunk and couldn't perform."

"Now, this may be important. Was Mattie willing?"

"Oh my God, no sir! The poor lass is engaged to be married. She came crying to me, clothes all torn, petticoats ripped off…She was a mess, she was. Took me nigh on to an hour to get her calmed down. Hastings came to the kitchen and fixed tea while I sat with her. The following mornin' when he went to Mr. Amesbury's room to lay out 'is clothes and tidy up as he usually does, 'e told the mister if it ever happened again the entire staff would quit and tell the missus why. Mr. Amesbury never bothered her again, did he?"

Pitt leaned his pipe against his tea saucer. A household within a household, or a family within a family. The household staff was a family of sorts in the home of the family they worked for, and in a subtle way, held sway over much of what went on in the home. He was sure the very thought of the entire staff quitting put the fear of God into Amesbury. Pitt smiled at the thought.

"Did anyone ever tell Mrs. Amesbury?"

"Oh no, sir. Hastings didn't think it was necessary."

"Well, I'm sure Hastings was right. And unless there's some good reason, I won't say a word either." Thinking of the moment's pause Mattie had made at the library door earlier, he added, "And I think it might be a good idea to tell Mattie not to say a word either. Your mistress has enough problems at the moment. She doesn't need more. You might also tell her you spoke with me about it."

"Aye, sir, I'll tell her."

"Thank you, Mary, and thank you for the tea. It was delicious."

The cabbie was wrapped in a rug and sound asleep inside the hansom when Pitt opened the door and startled him awake.

"Sorry 'bout that, Gov. Where we off ta?"

"Same as yesterday—just a few doors away to Dr. Cartwright's place."

"Right ya are, Gov." The cabbie started out the door to climb up on his seat, then stopped to reach inside and pick up a mug. "The butler brought me a hot cuppa while you was inside. I'll just set it on the step."

"Fine…What is your name, by the way?"

"Finny, sir, Alfred Finny, but most folks call me Fin."

"Alright, Fin, on to Dr. Cartwright's"

The rain had stopped but replacing it was a fog that seemed to swirl in layers along the road. Pitt sat back in the seat and relit his pipe. So now we have another person with motive, he thought. Mattie, after the attempted rape, could certainly have hated Amesbury enough to want him dead. As to opportunity, he wasn't sure, but would pursue that aspect of the case, if warranted, after he talked with Dr. Cartwright. He also assumed Inspector MacLeish didn't know of the incident or he would have heard. Come to think of it, other members of the household staff, in defense of Mattie, or retribution, may have taken it on themselves to end Amesbury's life. What a Pandora's Box! Then again, it was all conjecture with no proof.

The doctor was in a laboratory, dressed much as he'd been the day before, and though standing, bent over a large notebook resting on the edge of a lab table. He turned as Pitt entered the room.

"Ah…Mr. Pitt. Any further along in your investigation?"

"Very little, I'm afraid. I do have some medicines I'd like a professional opinion on, though." He produced the bottles taken from Amesbury's room and sat them next to the ones he'd received from Dr. Flack. "The two with the "P" on the label are mine. I visited Dr. Flack yesterday."

"I take it you complained of a sexual disorder?"

"Of the most distressful magnitude," said Pitt with a smile.

Cartwright looked him up and down, and smiled back. "You must certainly be an accomplished liar, Mr. Pitt."

"Truth be, I suspect Flack was more interested in money than diagnosis and cure."

"Well, an in-depth analysis might take some time. Do you want me to test for something specific or just provide a complete abstract of what I find?"

"I'd like to know if strychnine is found in any of the samples and in what quantity."

"That's simple enough. Have a seat and I'll ring for tea. The test for strychnine is rather straightforward. We dissolve a small amount of our sample in concentrated sulfuric acid in a test tube, place a few drops on a white porcelain tile, and add a small crystal of potassium dichromate and watch for a reaction. Depending on the strength of the strychnine, there will be produced at first, momentarily, a blue color, which quickly changes to purplish-blue, then gradually to violet, purplish-red, and cherry-red, and finally to orange or yellow." As he spoke, Cartwright added a bit of powder from the medicine bottles to four test tubes in a rack on the counter, added a liquid that Pitt assumed was sulfuric acid, shook each tube and replaced it in the rack.

Tea arrived and Pitt asked if a hot cup could be taken to his cabbie who was waiting outside. That arranged, he lit his pipe and watched as the doctor continued his analysis. All of the samples contained strychnine in varying degrees but the one found in Amesbury's room labeled "Prime" reacted most violently of the four.

"Why strychnine, doctor?"

"Oh, it does have its medical uses. Doctors will prescribe it in minute doses for several types of colic, heartburn or constipation. And while not proven, some, like your Dr. Flack, have used it to treat sexual disorders; though I am of the opinion that the effect is more mental than physical. It can cause slight contractions in the abdominal region that given the circumstance, could lead to arousal. I notice this last bottle is almost full, perhaps one dose missing. If Amesbury took a standard measure of it, the amount of strychnine in it would surely have killed him."

Pitt thought for a moment, taking short puffs on his pipe. "Could it have been mistakenly mixed at that strength, do you think?"

"Certainly it could have. Charlatans like Flack pay little heed to measures and such. It's the money that comes in the door, not the powders that go out, that are important to the likes of him. Are you saying Amesbury poisoned himself by accident?"

"I'm saying it's a possibility, perhaps even probable. I think I need to see Inspector MacLeish. I'll take the bottles with me but would you be willing to testify at a court of inquiry as to the results of this analysis?"

"Of course, but I doubt if it will be necessary if you give them to the Inspector. He'll have them tested again and a police chemist will testify. If I can be of any assistance, however, in any way, please have the good Inspector contact me. Speaking bluntly, Mr. Pitt, and of course off the record, Lucy is well rid of him, however it happened."

"From all I've heard, even from MacLeish, I would agree with you. Thank you for your time and expertise. I'll be glad to keep you informed of any developments if you like."

"Please do, and if you see Lucy later today, give her my best."

Anna, appearing like magic in the hallway and dressed in a brown sack-like dress as she'd been the day before, showed him to the door. "Your driver is ta kitchen havin' a cuppa. I'll send 'im round."

Pitt tapped the dottle from his pipe, refilled it, and was putting a match to the bowl when Fin came round the side of the house.

"Where to next, Gov?"

"The Yard, Fin. And take your time, the fog is getting worse." Pitt entered the cab, dropped the canvas blinds on all but one of the windows, and leaned back in a far corner to think. Given the analysis by Dr. Cartwright, accidental poisoning was a logical conclusion. Not only that, it might mean the arrest of Flack, though he wasn't sure on what charge. At the very least, it could be made too hot in London for him and he'd have to move on. Pitt suspected something similar might have happened in Australia and he might suggest it to MacLeish.

New and separate headquarters for the Metropolitan Police were built in 1890 along the Thames embankment and were referred to as New Scotland Yard, which is where they were headed. MacLeish shared an office with another inspector by the name of Bell, who Pitt knew, but not as well as MacLeish. He had the impression Bell was a plodder, slow and steady, but effective, whereas MacLeish tended to follow his instincts as much as the facts.

The hansom pulled over to the kerb and Pitt stepped out, turning to Fin as he did. Nodding to a group of hansoms gathered at the end of the block, he said, "You may as well wait. I should not be long."

"Right ya are, Gov. Ol' Fin'l be there."

Pitt entered the building and walked up to the second floor. He found MacLeish alone, bent over some papers laying on his desk, and mumbling to himself around the stem of a pipe than had gone out.

"That pipe works better if you light it."

The inspector glanced up and removed the pipe. "Aye, and would be even better if it had fresh tobacco in it."

Pitt laughed, took his tobacco pouch from his pocket and passed it to MacLeish who tapped the dottle from his pipe, refilled, and put a match to it. "Weel, what do ya have, laddie?"

Pit lit his own pipe. "You first, Mr. Mac."

"Fur openers, we've naught tae formally charge Mrs. Amesbury with but the intuition of an old inspector. Oh, we 'ave motive enough, wot with 'is well known loose behavior and the cruel way 'e treated 'er, but beyond that, no proof she did it. Searched that house 'igh an' low for strychnine, dint I, an' found nary a bit. Course, she coulda disposed of it somehow but no right after the event. No enough time, nor were she in the right place tae do it. I know ya be workin' for 'er lad, but 'ave ya turned up anything useful?"

"Maybe. Could be Amesbury killed himself."

MacLeish took the pipe from his mouth and sat down. "Stop for a pint or two on your way 'ere, did ya lad? The man is all set to tumble a whore and decides instead tae do 'isself in? You'd be getting' more than a smile from a court of inquiry on that one, laddie.

"In the first place, Mac, Amesbury may have been ready to bed a prostitute in his mind, but his plumbing wasn't up to the task. Ever hear of Dr. Flack?"

"Aye—Eastender. Deals in potions an' such. Might 'ave been responsible for the death of two prostitutes, but we've nowt proof, 'ave we? Was Amesbury seein' 'im?

"He was. And what's more, he had a couple of Flack's remedies in his WC. I went to Flack complaining of the same problem and got samples. Pitt then went on to relate his meeting with Dr. Cartwright and subsequent analysis of the contents of the bottles.

MacLeish tamped and relit his pipe. "Why is it, then, that Flack would put poison in 'is potions?"

"According to Dr. Cartwright, minute amounts of strychnine can cause contractions below the belt that might excite a man in the mood for sex, though his reaction is more in the head than the physical."

"So, you're sayin' Amesbury killed 'isself, accident like?"

"Probably with help from Flack, but it's unlikely you'll be able to prove it. He would simply claim anyone, including Amesbury, could have added more strychnine."

"Do ya have the potions wi' ya lad?"

Pitt took them from his coat pocket; two marked "P" and two marked "A". "I think your chemist will confirm Dr. Cartwright's analysis."

"I'll have them looked at immediately. And I'm thinkin' it's time I paid a wee visit to Dr. Flack. Would Mr. Pitt like to go along?"

"I think not. One visit was quite enough. I would like to know what you find, however. When is the inquest?"

"Tomorrow at nine o'clock. I expect you'd better be there."

"Wouldn't miss it."

It was more rain than snow falling when he left Scotland Yard, and the fog was thick and dun colored with a sulfur smell that caught in the throat. Fin was waiting inside the cab.

"Where we off ta, Gov?"

"Back to my place but I want you to take a note to Mrs. Amesbury and then return with her answer if there is one. In either case, I would like you to pick me up in the morning at eight o'clock."

"Right ya are, Gov. Fin's your man."

Returning to his rooms, Pitt asked Mrs. Keating for a fresh pot of tea, lit a pipe, then sat at his desk to write a note to Lucy.

Mrs. Amesbury,

There have been new developments that may clear you of any wrongdoing in your husband's death. Inspector MacLeish is looking into them and I expect to know the result in the morning, if not later today. I am otherwise engaged and find it impossible to return this afternoon, but will see you at the inquest tomorrow morning. No answer to this note is necessary. Best wishes, Joshua Pitt

---

There was a tap at the door and Mrs. Keating entered with a tray of tea and a sandwich. "I thought you mightn't the time for a meal, Mr. Pitt, so I fixed you a bite."

"You're an angel in disguise, Mrs. Keating, and a mind reader too. Thank you." He slipped the note in an envelope and handed it to her. "Would you mind handing this to the cabbie waiting outside? His name is Fin."

"He gave me his name when I took him a cuppa, before bringing yours up. Tis a cold job he has on days like this."

"That it is, Mrs. Keating, that it is. And thank you again."

Pitt wasn't otherwise engaged, as he'd told Mrs. Amesbury, at least not actively in the sense of this case or another. He simply wanted time to think. He couldn't shake the feeling he'd heard or overlooked something, or hadn't pursued a line of reasoning far enough. As he finished his sandwich, he walked to the window and looked down on Baker Street. It had stopped raining and a weak, late afternoon sun was poking its way through the haze. He felt the need for a walk and in any case, hadn't stopped by his tobacconist as he'd planned earlier. He finished his tea, slipped on his ulster, put two pipes in his pocket and picked up the tray to give to Mrs. Keating on his way out.

His tobacconist was located less than a mile away on Oxford Street, just several blocks off Hyde Park. There was chill and dampness in the air, and a pale yellow mist lay just above lamp level, providing a tunnel-like atmosphere to Baker Street as he walked.

All indications were that it was a case of self-poisoning, or at least self-administered—an accident brought about by incompetence on the part of Flack while preparing his tonics. Or was it? There wasn't a single shred of evidence otherwise. But the entire household, from Lucy to the servants, had ample reason to rid themselves of Amesbury. Any member of the household might have had opportunity to add strychnine to the bottle of Prime, but who would be most likely? Lucy, certainly, and Hastings. Mattie, of course, had perhaps more reason than anyone and could have slipped in unnoticed while doing her chores.

He turned left on Oxford Street, away from Hyde Park and continued his line of reasoning. But there was something else…Hastings. What was it Mary Waite had said while they had tea in the kitchen? That Hastings usually laid out Amesbury's clothes and tidied the room each morning. And it was Hastings who suggested to Lucy that Pitt should be called in. He found himself in front of Bradley Tobacconists at the same moment a sobering thought struck him: that he was quite possibly being manipulated by a very bright butler.

Pitt entered the shop and was immediately waved at by Mick, the senior clerk, who was waiting on another customer. He finished and came toward the front counter.

"Mr. Pitt—It's been a while since we've seen you."

"Too long. I'm out of Arcadia."

"Well, we can fix that. How much?"

"Four ounces—no, make it six. I want to give some to a friend. Any new pipes since I was last in?"

"Several Comoy's and Charatan's in the front case. No Peterson's though. Do you have a Charatan, Mr. Pitt?"

"No, I don't, but I've heard they're very good. I've seen Charatans at their shop but don't remember seeing them at other tobacconists. How is it you have some?"

"Aye, they are a bit expensive when compared to some others we keep in stock, but from time to time we manage to get several to sell. Shop owner to shop owner, so to speak, and the same is true for Comoy's and BBB."

Mick opened the case and laid four pipes on the counter. Pitt immediately reached for a medium sized pipe with apple shaped bowl. It was a natural color with thick tobacco chamber walls and straight, tapered stem. He picked it up.

"And how much for this gem, Mick?"

"You have a good eye. That's the best of the lot."

Pitt laughed. "I was afraid of that, but I'll take it anyway."

He paid for the pipe and tobacco, pocketed his purchase, and chatted a few minutes with Mick before leaving the shop. On the way back to his rooms, he decided a conversation with Hastings, after the inquest in the morning, might be worthwhile. More than worthwhile, perhaps.

He was walking up the stone steps to his boarding house when a hansom pulled to the kerb behind him and he turned in time to see Inspector MacLeish step to the sidewalk.

"Ho, laddie, ya comin' or goin'?"

"Just coming back from Bradley's. Would you like a cuppa?"

"Stronger, if ya 'ave it. Tis no been a good afternoon."

As they entered Pitt's sitting room, he motioned to a chair beside the desk and went to the cupboard for whiskey and glasses. He poured a strong tot for both, set the bottle on the desk, and sat down. He took a sip and set his new Charatan in the rack before selecting another pipe and lighting it.

"Looks like a new pipe, lad. Expensive one too."

"Charatan. Never had one before. Mick says they're a fine smoke."

"Well, it appears you'll be getting' paid for your efforts on behalf of Mrs. Amesbury, so you'll be able to afford another."

"You've arrested Flack?"

"We went tae 'is place of business an' was invited in real cordial like. I explained we were conducting an inquiry tae death of Arthur Amesbury by poisonin' an' since Amesbury were known tae be using the doctor's remedies, we wanted tae see the substances from which they was made. Twas was pretty much a mess, but we found several bottles of strychnine an' other questionable powders, includin' brucine, which I'm told is similar but less potent than strychnine. The good doctor, if tha's what he could be called, said it looked as though we'd be a while and he'd just step out the room a minute to tell 'is boy tae go home for the day. Five minutes later I went lookin' for 'im, only tae find 'ed buggered out the back. We 'ave a warrant for 'is arrest an' one of ours watchin' his place, but I doubt we'll get 'im soon. So, laddie, it looks as though you were right, dunt it? Amesbury dosed hisself wi' a bad batch o' Flack's powders."

"It certainly looks that way." Pitt took another sip of whiskey.

"Sounds like you're not too sure, lad."

"I thought it one possible solution and it's hard not to ignore the facts, as you're fond of saying, and Flack took off, which certainly points to his mixtures. It's also obvious that Amesbury took the mixture himself. Seems as though the case is closed. Another feather in your cap, Inspector."

"Aye. Well…I'm not quite comfortable wi' it, but it seems ta only answer. We'll be givin' testimony of tha' effect tomorrow."

"I'm sure Mrs. Amesbury will be happy to hear it." Not to mention her household staff, thought Pitt. "Would you like another whisky, Mac?"

"Thank ya, no. I'd better be getting' back tae Yard. Paperwork."

"Before you leave," said Pitt, picking up one of the packages of tobacco his desk and handing it to the Inspector. "I bought you a wee giftie when I was at Bradley's."

"Ya wouldna be tryin' tae bribe a man o' ta law, would ya laddie?"

Pitt was smiling. "I'd have no reason, now, would I?"

"No, I guess not. Thank ya, lad, I will enjoy this."

The coroner's inquest the following morning was brief and after the testimony of Inspector MacLeish, a verdict of death by misadventure was brought in. Afterwards, Pitt waited for Mrs. Amesbury and met her as she walked to her carriage. She was in the company of another woman and both were smiling.

"Mr. Pitt, this is Dr. Cartwright's wife, Sarah." Pitt smiled and touched the brim of his hat. "I was hoping to have a word with you, Mr. Pitt. Could you stop by the house this morning?"

"I'd be happy to. I'll follow in my cab." He turned and walked back to where Fin was waiting. "The Amesbury place, Fin."

"Right, Gov. On our way."

Pitt settled back in the seat and lit a pipe. It was cool and misty, but the sun was shining for a change and he relaxed, letting his mind wander. All's well that ends well, he thought, quoting Shakespeare. The Yard has closed their case, Lucy Amesbury wasn't charged, Flack is gone to parts unknown, and the world is rid of Amesbury, a sorry excuse for a man at best. The only one not quite satisfied was himself. Perhaps he never would be.

Hastings took his hat and coat and told him Mrs. Amesbury was in the library. As he turned to go, Pitt touched his arm. "After I speak with Mrs. Amesbury, would you have a cup of tea with me in the kitchen?"

Hastings paused, "If you like, sir. Mary will come get me."

Lucy was alone in the library and sitting in a chair near the fireplace. She motioned to Pitt to take a chair opposite her and he did so, while taking his pipe from his pocket and lighting it. As he sat down, she handed him a cheque and he glanced at it before setting it on the table between them.

"This is far too much, Lucy."

"No, it's not, Pitt. Without you, I'm sure I'd be in the dock charged with murder."

"And with a good solicitor, you'd be found not guilty. Whatever the Inspector thought, he had no proof of wrongdoing on your part."

"The point is, I'd be charged. It would be embarrassing, and no doubt scandalous, with the newspapers printing my husband's escapades daily. No, it is certainly worth it and more. Please accept it."

Pitt folded the cheque and put it in his pocket. "Since you put it that way, I will, but I will tell you honestly that I wasn't completely satisfied with the solution."

She looked surprised. "And why is that?"

"Flack was a charlatan and scoundrel of the first rank, but because of previous problems he may have had with the law in Australia, I suspect he took care to mix his potions properly. It seems unlikely he would have made a mistake of that magnitude. Why he fled, I suppose we'll never know."

"If not Flack, then who?"

"I honestly don't know. And it could well have been Flack's potion. In any case, it's a solution that has satisfied the law." Left unsaid was that it was a solution that satisfied a lot of others as well.

She was quiet for a moment, then smiled. "Well, you're right. It has satisfied the law and that's the important thing. I'd also like you to know that you're welcome here and it isn't necessary for you to be working for me. In fact, I hope never again."

"I hope so to, Lucy. Don't be surprised if I call from time to time. I think we'd enjoy each other's company in less stressful situations." He stood to go. "I'll be leaving now but I want to stop by the kitchen to say goodbye to staff. They were quite helpful."

She rose and extended her hand. "I meant what I said, Pitt, you're quite welcome here."

He took her hand. "I think I know that, Lucy."

When he walked into the kitchen, he was surprised to find Mattie, Mary, and Hastings, all having tea at the table. He sat down as Mary poured him a cup. He looked directly at Hastings. "Before entering service here, what did you do?"

"Army, sir. Twenty-two years. Sergeant Major before I was invalided out. Zulu war in Africa, sir, 1880."

"I suspected as much. Used to taking action then, in bad situations?"

"That I was, sir."

"That you *are*, Sergeant Major."

"Your meaning, sir?"

"I mean, that after Mattie here, was attacked by Amesbury, and the probable ongoing abuse of your mistress, you took action."

"And what action would that be, sir?"

"That would be a teaspoon or so of strychnine stirred into the top portion of the bottle of Prime that Amesbury kept in the cabinet of his WC. My guess is you did it during dinner or sometime before Amesbury came home. It doesn't really matter when, though I'm sure you had it worked out well in advance. A man does not attain the rank of Sergeant Major without superior intelligence and reasoning. You then suggested to Mrs. Amesbury that I be consulted, guessing that I'd spot the unusual potions in Amesbury's cabinet and have them analyzed. You must certainly have known of Flack's reputation and counted on him being held to blame. But since the coroner's jury found death by misadventure, there will be no further investigation. I simply want to know the truth for my own benefit."

Hastings looked at Mattie and Mary, took a sip of tea, smiled and said, "As you say, sir, I am used to taking action when confronted with what I perceive as a threat."

"And I assume that's the most direct answer I'll receive from you. Tell me though, does Mrs. Amesbury suspect anything other than what was ruled today by the coroner's jury?"

"No sir, she does not. And sir…I'm hoping you won't suggest otherwise."

Pitt relit his pipe and took several puffs before standing up to leave. "I have no reason to, Hastings. Thank you." He nodded to Mary and Mattie, and went to find Fin.

END

THE SHERLOCK HOLMES ADVENTURE

Joshua Pitt had just finished his last pipe of the evening, cleaned and put it in the rack, when he heard the sound of footsteps running lightly up the stairs to his third floor rooms. He waited for a moment till he heard tapping at his door. Opening it, he was surprised to see a young street arab of about 10 years, holding an envelope.

"You be Mr. Pitt?"

"I be," said Pitt, smiling. "What can I so for you, lad?"

"Mr. 'olmes give me a tanner to deliver this 'ere letter an' said you'd give me another when you read it."

Pitt took the envelope, opened it, and glanced quickly at the contents. Fishing in his pocket, he pulled out two thrupence and handed them to the lad.

"Aye lad, not a tanner but the same amount. Mr. Holmes was right. Thank you."

"Will there be a message, sir?"

"Tell Mr. Holmes I'll look into it."

The lad turned, ran as lightly down the stairs as up, while Pitt closed the door and went to his desk. He turned up the light, filled and lit a pipe, and then turned to the note from Sherlock Holmes. It read: "*Pitt—Inspector MacLeish paid me a visit this evening to discuss the particulars of a murder that occurred at Coldfall Lodge, Tetherdown. Mr. Artimus Weatherill was brutally murdered and property taken, including a fair amount in sovereigns.*

There are some particulars regarding this event that puzzle MacLeish and since I am returning to Glasgow in the morning to testify in the Seamus Walsh affair, I took the liberty of telling the Inspector you would look into it in my absence. If your appointments will give you the morning, MacLeish will be at Coldfell Lodge at seven o'clock. Best regards, Holmes"

There had been two other occasions since becoming an inquiry agent that he'd provided assistance to Sherlock Holmes, though Pitt had known him while a young lad running with the Baker Street Irregulars. Once was by accident when he discovered a client of his, Georges Lebec—a baker by trade—was providing safe haven for an assassin Holmes had been searching for. The second was soon after Holmes' return and while he was investigating the disappearance of Jonas Oldacre, the Norwood builder. The task was unrelated to Holmes' case but Pitt was asked to follow a senior bank clerk for three days and report his movements daily. It had resulted in the clerk's arrest along with two confederates who had been planning a robbery.

This Weatherill case was different. Pitt would not be providing assistance to Holmes, but acting in his stead, and he felt no mean pride in that. He had been asked to look into the matter by England's greatest consulting detective. It was an honor. It was also late and he needed to be fresh in the morning. He set his pipe in an ashtray, lit a candle, turned down the gaslight, and went to his bedroom. The morrow would be early.

Even before having his first cup of tea, he sent a boy to tell Fin he would need his services as a cabbie for the day. Alfred Finny had been a hansom driver most of his adult life and knew London and surrounding countryside better than most coppers. He also seemed to know most of London's unsavory characters, or at least knew about them, and was a valuable source of information.

Pitt had just lit his pipe and was standing on the boarding house steps when the hansom rounded the corner of Baker Street and pulled to the kerb.

"Mornin' Gov'nor, where we off ta this mornin'?"

"North London, Fin. Tetherdown—Coldfall Lodge, near the woods."

"Right, Gov. There's a wool rug on the seat 'n case ya feel ta coverin' up. The fog's middlin' but damp this mornin'."

"Thank you, Fin, I'll do that."

Pitt settled back in the seat, pulled the wool cover over his legs, and stared out the window while relighting his pipe. He sat on the pedestrian side of the hansom, listening to the rattle of the wheels on cobblestone, taking short puffs on his pipe. He was not familiar with the name of the deceased, nor for that matter, with Tetherdown and the Muswell Hill area, though a recent case had brought him to East Finchley, nearby. The area was one of large homes, wealthy inhabitants, and not known for much crime. A murder was rare. That usually indicated a family dispute but conjecture at this point, without facts, was useless. Better to simply enjoy his pipe and watch the passing scenery, what he could see of it through the mist, which was becoming heavier as they moved north.

There was a constable at the entrance to the winding driveway that led to the manor house. Pitt leaned out the window of the cab, gave his name and was told the Inspector was waiting for him. Inspector Angus MacLeish was an older Scotsman and long time member of Scotland Yard—a friend and fellow countryman of Pitt's. They had complimented each other on several cases, though Pitt refrained from taking credit for any contributions he might have made in solving them. Mr. Mac, or simply Mac, as Pitt often called him, was as steadfast and tenacious as a terrier with a meaty bone, but lacked imagination. His intuition, however, born of many years experience, made up for it.

The Inspector was standing in the doorway as the cab came to a stop at the steps of the manor house.

"Weel laddie, you be just in time for tea. PC Barnes is brewin' some in ta kitchen."

"It'll be welcome, Mac, there's a chill in the air this morning. Would you ask the constable to take a cup to my driver? I expect he could use it."

"Aye, laddie, I will do that. Come inside an' we can talk. I was still with Mr. Holmes last evenin' when his boy came back sayin' you'd come this mornin'. I appreciate it."

They walked to the kitchen, sat at the table, and both broke out their pipes. The constable sat mugs of tea in front of them and then took one to Fin.

Pitt noticed bloodstains on the floor and nodded to them. "Is that where you found the body, then?"

"Aye. 'E's been moved to the morgue. The gardener, one Henry Teague, found the front gate locked when 'e reported tae work yesterday morning and went round the wall to the garden entrance. When there was no response tae 'is knock at the front door, 'e went round tae the kitchen an' spied Weatherill sprawled on the floor. Not being able to get in through the door, he raised an alarm. We figure the fellow what did it forced the window above the sink but must have made some noise and woke old Weatherill who sleeps directly above. When 'e came down to investigate, 'e got 'isself bashed with a jemmy or pry bar. Smashed 'is skull. Dead afore 'e hit the floor, I expect. Everything is pretty much as we found it, 'cept for removing the body, of course."

"I don't know anything about Weatherill. Who was he?"

"Retired banker in 'is mid seventies an' in excellent health from all accounts. Might 'ave given a good account of hisself, if 'e 'ad the chance. Even though 'e were a banker, we 'ave it on good authority 'e kept a substantial amount of money on hand in a Chub upstairs in 'is bedroom. The gardener, a long time employee, as is the housekeeper, told me Weatherill paid them monthly in cash and that most of the business 'e conducted with local shops was in cash. And tha's the rub—there's no safe upstairs and no indication how it was got out of the house. No jewelry either, though I don't know at this point 'ow much 'e might 'ave had other than ta pocket watch Teague said 'e always carried."

"Could the assailant have carried the safe off?"

"Aye, perhaps, but I expect the safe 'ud weigh at least ten stone, an' it would take a stout lad to carry it any distance. There's no sign of it outside the house, at least not close by."

"Well Mac, let's take a look upstairs, shall we, and then we can have a look outside."

The upstairs of the manor consisted of a long hallway with doors to rooms at intervals on both sides. "There's a loo at each end of ta hallway, with one ta far end connecting with Weatherill's bedroom," said MacLeish as he led the way.

Pitt paused just inside the bedroom doorway and spent a moment absorbing the feel of the room before moving ahead. He sensed something wrong—out of place. No…Something out of balance was a more apt description. The floor was bare wood except for several small oriental rugs strategically placed on either side of the bed, one in front of the door to the WC, and one that cut an angle across the corner of the room to the left of the bed. The bed was a massive one of stout oak with posts at each corner. The covers were thrown back as if Weatherill had gotten up in a hurry. Pitt walked to the Oriental rug in the corner, bent to study it for a moment, and then walked to the corner of the bed nearest the WC. He ran his hand over the bedpost, then turned to MacLeish.

"How much of your investigation has been outside?"

"Enough ta determine the murderer tried two windows afore 'e got in through the kitchen."

Pitt entered the WC and opened the window. The grounds sloped away from the house toward a dense woods about one hundred yards distant. He ran a finger along the windowsill.

"Did you check as far as the woods?"

"Aye, as much as we could yesterday in the 'eavy fog. It promises tae be lighter today an' we'll give it another go."

Pitt walked back into the bedroom and to the corner next to the bed where he picked up the rug, looked at the floor underneath, and then ran his fingers over the wood.

"This is proving to be interesting, Mac. I think Mr. Holmes would have enjoyed looking into the matter. Let's go outside, shall we?"

Outside, and followed closely by constable Barnes, they walked the perimeter of the house, looking first at the two windows of attempted entry and finally at the kitchen window that was successfully levered open. Once, at a point between the first two windows, Pitt deviated from their intended path and walked fifty feet or so into the yard, then squatted down to look at the grass before returning. The inside hasp on the kitchen window was an old one and would have given way easily to a pry-bar, but not without some noise, which had probably alerted Weatherill as MacLeish surmised. After looking at the window, Pitt walked around the corner of the house to a point directly below the WC window, squatted again, and peered intently at the soft gray flagstone that formed a border for the flower bed that lay along side the house.

"Was Weatherill security conscious, Mr. Mac?'

"Weel, laddie, according tae the gardener, 'e had an alarm gun out ta far side of the garden but we 'aven't looked. I dint want my men stumblin' into it in ta fog yesterday."

"Then that's where they came onto the property."

"They?"

"Certainly, there were two. One inside and one outside. The inside man killed Weatherill, went upstairs to the bedroom and lowered the safe from the loo window. The rope he used wore a line in the paint on the sill. The safe was on the rug in the corner near the bed. I could see the outline of where it was because the rug was a slightly darker color where the safe normally sat. He slid the safe across the floor on the rug—I could see the marks left on the floor by his hobnailed boots—then tied a rope around the safe and using the bedpost like a single sheave block, lowered it through the window to the outside man. The bed was cocked slightly, having been moved away from the wall by the task. When the safe came down, a corner of it dug into the flagstone. Before leaving, the inside man placed the rug back in it's original spot, though I can't imagine why he bothered. I suspect you'll find the alarm gun has been disabled, and the safe, probably in the woods.

Inspector MacLeish stared at Pitt with an astonished look on his face. "I don't suppose you could describe the men—any distinguishing marks—anything like that?

Pitt laughed. "Sarcasm doesn't become you, Mac. I will tell you this, however. I suspect the inside man to be of average build but may walk with a slight limp. The scratches left by his right boot were more pronounced, therefore the right boot is more worn and the nails more exposed. I think your close examination of the grounds when the fog has lifted will bear me out."

"We shall see, me lad, but in truth, your examination 'as been helpful. How do you manage tae do that—that putting together of a criminal act?"

"To be honest, Mac, I'm not sure. Imagination is part of it I suppose. I put myself in the place of the criminal, set the task in my mind, and ask myself how I would do it. Then I mentally docket the answers in the order that seems logical. It doesn't always work out that way, but it does more often than not."

"My God, lad, between you an' Mr. Holmes…"

"Oh no, Mac, I'm not even in the same class as Sherlock Holmes. No detective living in England, perhaps even in Europe, is his equal. I'm quite honored he asked me to look in to this matter and provide some small assistance, but I am certainly not his equal, though I do thank you for the compliment."

"Quite welcome, I'm sure. You'll be leaving, then?"

"I think so. There's little else I can do here and you won't know much more till this afternoon when the fog lifts, if it does. Will you pay me a visit later? If not, please send me a note regarding anything additional you may find. This is an unusual case and it piques my interest."

"I will do that lad. A note, or a visit if not too late."

Pitt found Fin sitting on the front steps of the manor house, sipping tea and engaged in conversation with one of the constables.

"We'll be leavin' then' will we Gov?"

"We will, Fin. Back to my place and I don't expect to be needing you the rest of the day. I would appreciate it, though, if you'd come by in the morning—say about eight o'clock? And take your time going back. I have some thinking to do."

"Right cha are Gov'nor. Ol' Fin'll take 'er slow."

For whatever reason, Pitt oft-times thought best while riding in a cab, puffing on his pipe while tucked back in a corner, watching London slip by the window. He didn't know why, any more than he knew why the solution to some cases came to him intuitively, though the absence of facts might leave gaping holes in the thought process. Much like chess, given the opening, he could often predict the direction the game would take and occasionally the outcome. Such might not be the case with the Weatherill affair, however. The opening was rather straight forward. Two men, for there were two, surely, had broken into Weatherill's home and one had bludgeoned him to death while the other waited outside. Pitt had pointed MacLeish in the right direction and doubted he could do anything more. Doubted, as well, that the two would be caught. He could picture them carrying the safe to the woods where they opened it, took whatever was inside of value, and then probably hoofed it back to the east end to disappear in the throngs and rabbit warrens of half a million people.

This wasn't a simple burglary, however. It had been compounded by a needless murder and that's what bothered Pitt. Most burglars, if discovered, would break for the open road, not murder the person who caught them breaking in. Unless...unless, of course, they were known to the person who caught them. It made sense and was a line of inquiry that deserved to be pursued. He would suggest it to MacLeish.

As he got out of the cab, he reminded Fin he would need him the following morning and then, instead of climbing the steps to his own rooms, he walked north on Baker Street to 221. Mrs. Hudson answered his knock.

"Why, Mr. Pitt, we've not seen you for a while, have we?"

"No ma'am. Is Mr. Holmes in?"

"He's been delayed in Glasgow and will be two more days there. Dr. Watson is upstairs, though. You can go right up. I'll bring tea."

The door opened to his knock. Dr. Watson, with pipe in mouth and a copy of the *Times* in his hand smiled a greeting.

"Joshua—Good to see you! Come in, come in. Holmes is away at the moment, in Glasgow for two more days at last report."

"Good to see you too, John. Mrs. Hudson told me he'd been delayed up north."

"Well, have a seat by the grate and fill me in on what you've been doing lately. There's some Arcadia in the roll-up pouch on the table. Help yourself."

Pitt took a pipe from his pocket, filled it with tobacco, then took a seat in front of the fireplace before lighting up. "As you probably already know, Mr. Holmes asked me to look into the Weatherill murder in Tetherdown and provide whatever assistance I could to Inspector MacLeish, though Mac is rarely in need of help."

Pitt went on to tell what he'd uncovered, his hypothesis as to the nature of the crime and his suspicion that the two men knew or had worked for Weatherill at one time. He'd just finished relighting his pipe when a tap at the door brought in Mrs. Hudson with tea and freshly baked scones—a welcome sight. Pitt was hungry.

They continued to discuss the case while eating and when finished, Watson sat back in his chair and relit his pipe. "So, Joshua, what's your next step? Do you intend to pursue it further?"

"That may well depend on whether MacLeish feels the need for additional assistance or if he thinks he has the case in hand. I expect him to drop by this evening but other than conjecture, I'm not sure I have more to offer."

"Well, one thing my time with Holmes has taught me is that conjecture often leads to resolution, but I have to admit that he is more often closed mouth about it than not. Tell me though; you've speculated these men may have worked for Weatherill at one time. If that's true, they may well have known the habits of the man and the routine of the household. How is it then, they plan a robbery when the likelihood of discovery is high? They took the safe from the old man's room which surely meant confrontation, but as it happened, that occurred in the kitchen."

Pitt set his pipe on the table and took a sip of tea. "That's true, but perhaps they were simply casual labor and didn't know the household all that well. Then again…it could well be that murder was their original intent and robbery, the tart that sweetened the deed."

Watson relit his pipe and took several short puffs. "I agree with you, that the likelihood of finding them is slim unless additional information is forthcoming."

Pitt stood and pocketed his pipe. "I'd better be getting back to my place. I'm not sure what time MacLeish intends to visit but I'd like to be there. Thank you for the conversation and suggestions, John, and please thank Mrs. Hudson for tea."

"You're welcome, I'm sure. I'll tell Holmes of our speculations when he returns. I'm sure he'll be interested."

"You might add that I think there is nothing more to be done at this point. At least I can't think of anything."

Mrs. Keating, his landlady, was sweeping the stairs as he came in. "Will you be having tea, Mr. Pitt?"

"Thank you, but no. I just had tea with Dr. Watson. Has Inspector MacLeish been by to see me?"

"No, but a boy came by with a note for you. I put it on the desk in your sitting room. The lad didn't say who it was from."

He saw the envelope on his desk as he entered the room but first took the pipes from his pocket, set them in a tray and then hung up his coat and hat. He poured himself a whiskey, added a bit of water, then sat at the desk and opened the envelope. The note was short: "*Laddie—As you suspected, we found the alarm gun disabled and just inside the edge of the woods, we found the Chub, which were expertly opened. If there were anything of value it were taken, leaving only a few unimportant papers and a small packet of letters. There were two sets of footprints as you also surmised and we were able to follow them for a short distance in the direction of Tetherdown Lane but lost them in the leaves and underbrush. I will be by early evening if at all possible. MacLeish*"

Pitt read the note through a second time and then set it aside to fill and light a pipe. There was nothing new in the note and unless some new development occurred, he doubted the murder would be solved. Thinking it would be at least an hour before MacLeish arrived, he took the opportunity to review his account books. They were not account books in the ordinary sense, though they did track expenses and receipts from cases he worked on as well as his bank balance. More than that, however, they also included notes on his cases with names, dates, impressions, conjecture, and final outcome. He had slightly over 900 pounds in his account. A tidy sum, but he mentally noted that the bulk of it came from two recent cases and most from the Amesbury affair. The lesser addition came from the recovery of both wife and blackthorn walking stick of an Irish nobleman, though as he remembered, the nobleman cared more for the stick than the wife.

His pipe had gone out and he rested it against the edge of a small four-pipe rack he kept on his desk. He smiled as he looked at the rack. In it was a new pipe, a large Charatan, still unsmoked, that he'd bought some weeks before. As his income increased, so had his collection of pipes which now numbered over thirty. His selection of tobaccos had increased as well, much to the pleasure of Inspector MacLeish who saw the largess as an opportunity to sample new blends without spending a few shillings.

On a clean page in his ledger, he wrote the heading, *Assist Holmes—Weatherill* and wrote a couple of paragraphs outlining the case. He was just closing the book when there was a knock at the door.

"That you, Mac?"

"Aye laddie."

"Come in—it's open."

The door opened and MacLeish, in tweeds and a bowler hat, stepped into the room. His dark beard, flecked with grey, was shining with the moisture of an evening fog. He was a big man but moved with surprising lightness and ease to a chair in front of the desk, removed his bowler, and pulled a pipe from his pocket.

"I took ta liberty of askin' Mrs. Keating tae send her boy for a pitcher of beer from ta Quail. Tis been a dry day, in a manner of speakin'."

Pitt smiled. "I suppose you'd like a bowl of tobacco with your beer?"

"Aye, tha' would be nice."

Pitt pushed a glass container half full of tobacco toward the inspector. "Some Gawith Stoved Virginia here, or there's some others on the sideboard if you'd like something different."

"Nay, this'll be fine." He filled his pipe, lit it, then sat back in the chair, smiling. "Tha' were a fine bit o' work you did this mornin'. Looked good in my report, it did. Your name didn't appear, as you like, but I wouldna mind if it did."

"There's no reason it should. And from time to time you've helped me by providing information I couldn't get anywhere else. So…did you turn up anything new?"

"Not much, though PC Barnes is thinkin' he's seen the manner in which the Chub was opened somewhere afore. An' I've put out some feelers in the east end and docklands. Simple thievery won't be gettin' any response but murder might."

"Any idea how much they got?"

"Weel, wages was due the staff an' it were time tae fill the larder. We're gussin' o' course, but nigh on tae fifty pounds, an' according tae staff there were some family jewels kept in the safe. Some jade pieces an' a gold necklace. There were also Weatherill's gold pocket watch. Dealin' o' course, they'd only get a quarter o' worth."

There was a knock at the door and Mrs. Keating entered carrying a large ceramic pitcher and a towel. "The gentleman's beer, sir."

"Thank you, Mrs. Keating. On the sideboard will be fine."

"Will the gentleman be staying for dinner? I'll be having ham and boiled potatoes with fresh baked bread."

Pitt looked at MacLeish and raised an eyebrow. "Well, what say you, Inspector? Join me for dinner?"

"Aye, an' thank you for ta kind offer, ma'am. Tis nowt that I get a home cooked meal an' Mr. Pitt is always complimentin' your cookin'."

Mrs. Keating blushed as she turned toward the door. "It will be ready in about half an hour, sir. I'll bring it up."

"No need, Mrs. Keating. We'll come to the kitchen."

"Very good, sir."

For the next twenty minutes they discussed the case and Pitt told of his visit, conversation, and speculations with Dr. Watson. The Inspector filled his glass a second time, relit his pipe and stared blankly at Pitt's desk for a moment.

"I'm tinkin' we'll need a beak wi' this one, Laddie, at least if we 'ave any 'ope of clearin' it up quickly. Weatherill did 'ire some day labor tae turn the garden or do some paintin' on occasion, but there's nowt a record of names. I'll be talkin' wi' some snitches in the East End o'er the next couple o' days but it's unlikely tae turn anything." His eyes shifted to the pipe rack on Pitt's desk. "I see you've bought a new pipe."

"About a week or so ago." Pitt took the pipe from the rack and handed it to MacLeish. "It's a Charatan, but as you can see, I haven't smoked it yet. Maybe in the next day or so…" His voice trailed off. He realized the pipe was an indication of financial success, albeit on a small scale, and that a policeman's salary didn't lend itself to expensive pipes. He doubted the Inspector had more than four briars, and common ones at that.

"Aye, it's a nice piece an' should be a pleasure to smoke." He handed it back to Pitt who put it in the rack and then stood.

"I expect we should be going downstairs. Supper should be ready."

They pocketed their pipes and MacLeish picked up the beer pitcher. "No sense leaving this behind, ya tink, Lad?"

Pitt laughed. "None at all, Mac, none at all."

After they'd supped, and after MacLeish left, Pitt sat at his desk sipping a small whiskey and pondering the case, but nothing new came to him so he finally gave up. Thinking he'd read for a while, he went to his bookcase, selected a thin volume of Kipling, filled and lit a pipe and returned to his desk. Within a few moments, he realized how tired he was, set pipe and book aside, finished the last few drops of whisky and headed for bed. Perhaps he'd put a few feelers of his own out tomorrow.

He was awake betimes, had finished his toilet and was filling a pipe when there was a tap at the door.

"Come in, Mrs. Keating."

She entered carrying a small tray with tea and scones. "Your cabbie is downstairs. He said he knew he was early but that he'd woke at the crack of dawn; though how he could see it is beyond me. There's a thick, yellow fog this morning."

"I hadn't looked, but thought as much. I could smell the heavy coal smoke. Ask Fin to come up, would you? And hand him a cup on his way."

Fin entered the room, cup in one hand, cap in the other, and looked around. He'd never been in Pitt's rooms before.

"Nice place you 'ave 'ere Gov'nor."

"Thank you, Fin," said Pitt, rising from his desk and picking up the teapot. "Come over near the fireplace and have a seat." They sat in front of the coal fire, Pitt poured for both of them and then lit his pipe.

"This Weatherill case is a stumper, Fin, and I don't think the motive was robbery. I think it was a planned murder and the robbery was a bit of bonus for the two who did it. Has there been any chaff on the streets about it?"

"Nary a word, Gov. If it were just robbery, they'd be bullyrag, but murder's a hangin' offence and them wot did it ain't likely to brag on it. A copper friend did tell me they was expert cracksmen, though. Opened tha' Chub like it were a rusty tin, dint they?

"I'll not be going out this morning but I'd like you to do me a favor and I'll pay you for your trouble. I suspect the two who murdered Weatherill have gone to ground in the East End, Dockside, or some other rabbit warren. I'd like you to prowl about and gather what information you can. Pick up a fare or two and stop at some pubs if you like, but report back here by mid afternoon. Will you do that?"

"Aye, Gov, that I will."

As Fin got up to leave, Pitt handed him a Sovereign saying, "That should cover expenses and then some, but if you have to use some of your own money, tell me. Information may cost you something."

Fin laughed. "That it may, Gov, but it's unlikely to cost mor'n a pint."

Pitt walked Fin to the door and as he opened it, a young lad came running up the stairs. "Telegram for Mr. Pitt."

"That would be me, lad."

The boy handed over the telegram, accepted some pennies, and ran lightly down the stairs ahead of Fin.

Pitt relit his pipe, which had gone out, sat at his desk, and unfolded the telegram. It had no salutation, but simply read: "*Telegram received from Watson regards your findings and speculation on the Weatherill affair thus far. I am not surprised there is little to go on, though your hypothesis of murder as the first intent seems most likely. You must play a waiting game, perhaps. There are times, my dear Pitt, when the most intelligent something you can do is nothing. ...Holmes*"

He smiled and imagined Holmes must have done the same as he wrote it. Holmes was right: sometimes a waiting game is the best course to follow. Still-hunting sometimes brings the hunted animal to your feet. He considered a reply but since one was not prepaid for, assumed none was expected, which told him Holmes would probably return to London on the morrow. It would be nice if Pitt had more to offer by then, but didn't have high hopes.

Without much else to do and no other cases on his calendar, he decided a walk in near-by Regents Park might be in order. His best thinking was often while walking, and oft-times in sour weather. He peered out the window and saw the fog had lifted somewhat but not enough that the gas lamps had been damped. After slipping into his ulster and soft wool cap, he pocketed two pipes and tobacco pouch. Pausing at the door, he picked a stout blackthorn walking stick from the umbrella stand. One never knows...

Pitt entered the park at Hanover Gate, crossed the outer circle road, and then followed the path along the boating lake. The fog seemed thinner at ground level than it had from his window, yet visibility was hardly more than fifty feet and the mist formed layers of varying thickness over the water. There were few people about and he saw no ducketts, as Molly Brick was wont to call the tea and biscuit venders that plied their trade along the paths of the park. He smiled, thinking of Molly, something he hadn't done for quite a while. She'd brought him his second or third case, he couldn't remember which, offhand; one that had a happy, if not humorous ending.

He'd walked perhaps a quarter mile and was close by the footbridge that crossed one of the fingers of the lake when he decided to sit on a convenient bench and light a pipe. There was a small island just a few feet offshore at this point and the footbridge arched just enough to permit the passage of punts that rowers hired from a concessionaire at the far end of the lake. He was just putting a second match to his pipe when he heard angry voices, one male and one female.

He could make out two dark shapes coming over the bridge, though being off to one side on the bench, he doubted they could see him. Near the end of the bridge, the man stopped and spoke to the woman's back as she continued to walk.

"You should marry 'im, you bitch! 'E's got money, hadn't 'e?"

Without turning, she answered in a loud voice. "Can't even get it up, can 'e? Older'n me grandma, in't 'e?"

"Aye, but tha's the point! The old cove could die at any time after, convenient like, if you'll be listenin' ta me. Couple a months..."

"Couple a months of a weak joint punchin' at me! Cor! I've picked better things outta my nose!"

Pitt stifled a laugh. He had to admit he hadn't heard that one before.

She was turning left off the bridge, away from Pitt, when the man caught up with her, spun her around and pinned her to the wood railing. He raised his hand

and she ducked but he didn't strike. Instead, he grabbed the front of her coat and shook her viciously. "You listen to me, sister o' mine! Tha old Barrister 'as takin' a likin' ta ya, 'adn't 'e? 'E gets ta swillin' tha plonk an' proposes, dun't 'e? 'Im wi' money up the arse an' you turn 'im down. Well, your 'bout ta 'ave a change of 'eart, or so 'elp me God, you'll be greetin' Jesus afore 'e does!"

The fog had shifted slightly and in the yellow light, Pitt could make them out somewhat. She wasn't unattractive, perhaps in her mid twenties, with red hair that tumbled to her shoulders from below a narrow scarf. The fear on her face was patent and it was obvious she took her brother seriously. Her brother was broad shouldered, bearded, with large ham-like hands that gathered in most of the front of her coat. A countryman perhaps, or a laborer, and from his accent, from the Midlands, most probably. Pitt immediately dismissed the thought of interfering unless it appeared murder was immanent, which he thought unlikely.

The brother had loosened his grip and the woman turned slightly toward the path speaking louder as she did. "Alright, alright, I'll make up to the auld sod, but I'll no be puttin' up wi' 'is pawin' an' foul breathin' on me for donkey's years."

The brother let go of her coat and in a soft voice that Pitt could barely make out, said, "Maude, you marry this cash cow, an' you'll be a grievin' widow a few fortnights after. I promise ya."

"Aye, and transported a fortnight after that."

"You'll no go to prison, I promise ya. Coppers'll nowt be blamin' a widow for an accident, can they?"

"What kind of accident?"

"Leave tha' ta me. No need ta be knowin'."

As they turned and resumed their walk along the path, she took his arm and their voices faded as they disappeared in the mist. Pitt was tempted to follow but thought better of it. Whatever was planned was several months away if marriage was involved and he had enough information that he could probably identify the Barrister with a few inquiries. That is, if he chose to pursue it, which he probably would. At the very least, he could ask Inspector MacLeish about any drunken, retired member of the bar that was given to taking up with a red headed strumpet named Maude.

His pipe had gone out. He tamped the ash with his finger and relit. He'd come here to think about Weatherill and had been interrupted by the little episode by the bridge. Whatever thoughts he might have had, had flown with Maude and her brother. In any case, he had little information to go on, and rehashing what he knew would most likely get him nowhere. Sometimes though…Sometimes a walk in the close nether world of fog would open doors to other paths of inquiry. Not this time, however. He decided to walk back to his rooms and wait on Fin to return. Perhaps the cabbie would have something useful.

He pocketed his pipe and had only taken a few steps when he heard what seemed to be a young boy's voice calling his name.

"Mr. Pitt! Mr. Pitt!"

"Over here, lad, by the bridge!"

It was Mrs. Keating's boy, who must have made the half circle around the lake at a run because he was out of breath.

"What is it, lad? Is Mrs. Keating alright?"

"Yes sir…she is that…it's your police friend, sir…He's been shot."

On their way back to the house, the boy told Pitt what he knew. Fin had returned early after hearing MacLeish had been shot while questioning a man in the East End. The boy didn't know MacLeish's condition, only that Fin knew which hospital he'd been taken to and was waiting for Mr. Pitt.

True to the lad's word, Fin was sitting atop his hansom in front of the boarding house and Mrs. Keating was on the steps wrapped in a shawl. She turned in his direction as he and the lad appeared quickly out of the fog.

"I sent the boy soon as Fin told me, Mr. Pitt."

"Thank you Mrs. Keating. Reward the boy with some tea and something sweet."

Fin picked up the reins. "Climb up 'ere sir, next ta me. I can be tellin' ya wha' I know as we go."

Pitt stepped on the wheel and hoisted himself onto the seat next to Fin. "Which hospital is he in and how bad is he hurt?"

"They took 'im ta St. Bart's. Don' know 'ow bad. I know 'e were shot by some cove 'e were askin' questions of. 'E were in Shadwell near Whitechapel an' I'd just come from dockside when I seen ta crowd. I pulls over an' asks some tart what's standin' there wi' a gin in 'er paw, an' she says a copper'd been shot. I get down and walks ta the crowd just as they go ta loadin' 'im in a cab an' I sees it's your friend ta Inspector. I asts the PC where they was takin' 'im, an' the PC says St. Bart's."

Within ten minutes, they arrived in front of St. Bartholomew's hospital and Pitt dismounted, telling Fin to pull the cab off to the side and wait. Having never been inside St. Bart's, he wasn't sure where to go but walked down the long main corridor with rooms and offices running off each side till he came to an alcove. It appeared to be a dispensary of sorts and a Sister was sitting at a desk.

"Can you tell me, Sister, if a police officer was brought in a short time ago? He's been shot and I'd like to know his condition."

"I don't have an answer to either question. What's his name and are you related to him?"

The question took Pitt off guard but without pause, he answered, "His name is Angus MacLeish, and I'm his brother, Joshua." He could always apologize for the lie later, but for now, finding out how badly MacLeish was hurt was more important.

"Please wait, sir, and I'll inquire. She rose from behind the desk and Pitt was surprised at how tall she was, perhaps five foot nine, slender, and with an aristocratic carriage that spoke more of Bond Street than St. Bart's. As she walked through the hallway door, he though of how the day had been full of surprises. He also wondered how female nursing staff at hospitals had acquired the title of *Sister*. To him, it seemed like an odd title and he made a mental note to ask someone if the opportunity arose. She was gone perhaps three minutes and when she returned, held the door open for him.

"I'm told your brother's wound doesn't appear to be serious. If you follow me, I'll take you to see him."

"Thank you, Sister. Ummm…if you don't mind my asking, what is your name?"

She smiled. "No, Mr. MacLeish, I don't mind. It's Langston, Elizabeth Langston."

They went through the door, down a short hallway and then turned left into another. She stopped at the third ward and opened the door. He stepped past her and the faint scent of lilac attracted his attention as he mumbled his thanks.

MacLeish was in the third bed with a screen at the side and foot. He had his eyes closed and appeared to be sleeping but as Pitt approached the open side of the bed, the Inspector opened one eye.

"Ya didna bring a pipe w' ya, by any chance, laddie?"

"I did. Two, to be exact, but I wouldn't think they'd allow smoking in the ward."

"Most likely wouldn't taste good anyway, would it?"

"What happened, Mac?"

"I was doon ta Dockside checkin' a tip on the Weatherill case. I 'ad word some cove, name of Jack Poston, and another fellow was tryin' tae work a deal on some baubles he 'ad, an' among them was a gold pocket watch. Now, Poston 'as a long record o' thievin' and I 'appen tae know 'e was released from Newgate Prison two weeks ago. Seems 'e an' another bloke were convicted of stealin' tools some months back while in the employ of a certain Mr. Weatherill. Inspector Bell an' meself tracked 'im to the *Rose And Thorn* but when I was aboot tae confront 'im, 'e pulled a Bulldog an' fired from across a table. If it hadna been 'e was risin' from a chair an' tripped, 'e would a 'ad me square. As it were, the bullet raked me right side but dint break any ribs. I'll 'ave a score to settle wi' tha' right bastard, though I'm guessin' 'e scarpered out ta city by now."

"So you're going to be alright, then. Will they be keeping you here for a while or will the doctor allow you to go home this evening?"

"Doctor dint say a word, but yon nurse told me two days 'ud be fair tae watch for infection and make certain ta wound is healin' proper. By the by, 'ow'd you you 'ear of me bein' shot?"

Pitt pulled his pipe from his pocket and put it in his mouth, forgetting for a moment he was in a hospital. He took it out and held it in his hand. "Fin was only a block away from you when it happened, asked where they were taking you, and came to get me."

"If you light that pipe, laddie, will you share it wi' me?"

"I'd be happy to but I think it would get us both in trouble. We'll share a bowl and a whiskey when you get out."

"I'd be a happy man wi' a pint o' Guinness. Now, if ya think you could be sneakin' one in…" He laughed and then groaned. "When I get me hands on tha' bastard Poston, I'll be savin' a hangman trouble."

They talked for a few minutes more and then Pitt took his leave, stopping for a moment in the dispensary alcove on his way out.

"Miss Langston, I'm afraid I have a confession to make. I'm not Inspector MacLeish's brother, just a close friend. I don't like a lie, for that's what it was, and I apologize."

"Apology accepted but I must tell you I didn't believe you after I'd seen the Inspector. Even with a different mother or father, there's no likeness at all and he's certainly twenty or more years older than you. If you don't mind, what is your real name?"

"Pitt, Joshua Pitt."

"Well, Mr. Pitt," she said, smiling, "I don't like participating in a conspiracy but if you plan to return, and if there's a problem, you may continue to be the Inspector's brother, though I'm afraid you'll have to speak out on your own. I won't lie for you."

"Thank you." He hesitated. "May I ask; is pipe smoking permitted in the ward?"

"As much as I enjoy the aroma of a pipe, it is not permitted, though patients and visitors may step out in the solarium at the far end of the corridor if they like."

"If you have the opportunity, you might let the Inspector know that."

"I will, and good day to you, Mr. Pitt."

After relating to Fin what had occurred and telling him the Inspector would recover, he spent the short ride back to his rooms puffing on his pipe and thinking about the incident. Having shot a copper, Jack Poston had put himself in a precarious position. Not only would every policeman in England be looking for him, but as was normal, a reward upwards to one hundred pounds would be offered for information and capture. Since that amount of money was more than many Londoners made in a year, chances of some poor beggar peaching on Poston were high. And for that reason, Poston would either go to ground in the rabbit warrens of the East End or Docklands, or get out of London. Perhaps both, in that order. Pitt had friends and contacts in the East End, Whitechapel, and other less desirable areas of London, but not what could be called an established network of informants.

By the time they reached Baker Street he'd smoked his pipe to the bottom of the bowl and it had gone out. He tapped the remaining ash into his hand and dumped it in the street before turning to Fin to hand him a five pound note.

"Take your fare and expenses out of this, Fin, and use the remainder to gather what information you can about Poston. In particular, I want to know two things: is he still in London, and who his mates are. Be as liberal with your funds as need be and come back to me for more if you need it. A word of caution: he's murdered one man and shot a copper. If you discover where he's gone to ground or in the unlikely event you spot him, simply return to me. One friend in St. Bart's is enough."

"Right you are, gov'nor. Will you be needin' Fin any more today?"

"No, I don't think so, but come by tomorrow morning before making your rounds and you can take me to the hospital."

Fin touched the brim of his hat and moved off down the street as Pitt walked up the steps of his boarding house. Mrs. Keating was coming down the hallway as he started up the stairs to his room.

"Is your policeman friend going to be alright, then?"

"It was a minor wound, if being shot can be called minor in any way. He should be on the mend and out of hospital in a day or two."

"Ah now, that's good to hear. Have you eaten, Mr. Pitt?"

"I have not, and even in the hallway here, I smell something spicy."

"Curried lamb with rice. I'll bring some up to your rooms with a pot of tea if you like."

"That would be wonderful, Mrs. Keating, and thank you."

He entered his sitting room and after hanging up his coat and hat, selected a pipe from his rack, filled it, and then poured himself a whiskey. He was sitting at his desk staring at the new, unsmoked Charatan pipe he'd bought the week before when there was a tap at the door and Mrs. Keating came in carrying a tray.

"You can tuck into this, Mr. Pitt, and there's more in the kitchen."

He surveyed the heaping mound of rice and lamb with what looked like a fourth of a loaf of bread on top and smiled. "I think this will be quite enough, and thank you again."

He usually took his suppers in the dining room or kitchen but on occasion, Mrs. Keating sensed when he'd prefer the privacy of his room and thoughts. Though it only consisted of two rooms, his apartment was decorated to his liking, comfortable, and sufficient to his needs. The sitting room, which he called his office, was actually quite large with table and chairs, two comfortable wingbacks near the fireplace, and his desk near the outside wall next to ample bookshelves. From his front window, he could look down of Baker Street, and from his bedroom, he could see the trees of Regent's Park. He finished his whiskey, set his pipe aside, poured a cuppa, and *tucked in*, as Mrs. Keating would say.

He had finished his meal, relit his pipe, and was taking a sip of tea when there was a knock at the door.

"Come in, please." It was Mrs. Keating.

"A lad just came with a note for you, sir. He didn't wait for a reply." She handed him a small, unsealed envelope that simply had **J. Pitt** written on the front of it.

"Thank you, and thank you for a delicious supper."

"I brought *The Times* for you as well. Will you be wanting more to eat?"

"No, Mrs. Keating, it was quite enough."

She gathered up the plates, put them on the tray, and then asked if he'd like more tea. He told her no, but to leave the pot. He'd bring it downstairs later. She left and he turned to the note. It was from John Watson.

> "Joshua, Holmes returned late this afternoon, arriving just minutes before we received news of MacLeish being shot. He has gone out again but asked me to contact you in hopes you would be free to visit our rooms tomorrow morning at nine o'clock. He will assume you are able to do so unless he receives a note from you in the morning to the contrary. Regards, John"

Smiling, Pitt reread the note and then set it aside. More of a summons than a request, he thought, but typical Sherlock Holmes. He'd planned to visit MacLeish in the morning but would put it off till later in the day. He poured himself more tea and opened *The Times*. At the bottom of the front page was a small item about MacLeish, though it didn't give the inspector's name. *The Times* had probably just received some sketchy information but a policeman being shot was important enough to merit the front page of the newspaper. It was only a half dozen lines saying a Scotland Yard Inspector had been shot while attempting to apprehend a suspect in a criminal matter. Not much else.

With nothing pressing, a quiet evening with the newspaper, a bowl or two of tobacco and a late whiskey, would be welcome. He yawned. He might even pass on the whiskey and simply go to bed early after returning Mrs. Keating's teapot.

It was still dark when he woke. Either that, or the fog was so thick the light from the streetlamp wasn't shining dimly through the muslin curtains of his bedroom as usual. He got up, slipped on his robe, parted the curtains and looked at his pocket watch. It was both: the grey-brown fog was so thick he could barely make out the diffused glow of the streetlamp and his pocket watch said it was a few minutes before six. He put his slippers on, filled a pipe and put it in his pocket, and went downstairs to the kitchen. Mrs. Keating was just putting water on to boil for tea.

"You're an early riser this morning, Mr. Pitt."

"Went to bed early last night. I'm expecting Fin this morning to take me to the hospital but will be seeing Sherlock Holmes instead. In this fog, it's unlikely he'll arrive before I leave. Would you tell him to come by early afternoon?"

"I will, that. I think I asked yesterday, but will your friend be in hospital long?"

"I expect they'll send him home tomorrow with orders to rest for a few days, but I doubt that he will—rest, that is. He's an angry man and will be anxious to go after the man who shot him. Can't say as I blame him."

"Nor I. Would you like a pot of Assam to take upstairs or do you want a cuppa here in the kitchen?"

"A pot would be nice, Mrs. Keating. Thank you."

He returned to his rooms, completed his toilet, dressed and then relaxed near the fireplace with pipe and tea while he read through the morning's copy of *The Times*. He enjoyed reading the *Personals*, or as Holmes called them, the agony columns. For Pitt, they simply provided a glimpse into a few of the lives of the several millions who inhabited London, but to Holmes, they were often the beginning, or the end, of another mystery. At ten minutes to nine, he set the newspaper aside, selected a pipe from his rack, donned his ulster, started out the door and then stopped. He went back to his desk, picked up the new Charatan pipe he'd bought the week before, and put it in his inside coat pocket. The streets were fog shrouded and the short walk to 221B was in a typical steady, cold London rain. Mrs. Hudson answered the bell and he climbed the stairs, stopping at the top to knock. As he raised his hand, Holmes' voice came from the other side of the door.

"Come in, Pitt, the door's open."

Holmes, wearing a heavy, quilted robe, was sitting near the fire, one foot propped on the fender and puffing gently on a pipe. A copy of *The Daily Post* was lying on his lap, open to the Personals columns.

"I know," said Pitt, smiling, "the good doctor has often commented you know the sound of his footsteps on the stairs, but how did you know it was me?"

"Quite simple. Watson was standing by the window drinking his coffee and said, 'I think I see Joshua coming through the rain and fog.' I simply waited till I heard you stop at the door. Hand Watson your coat and hat and he'll hang them up to dry."

Pitt took pipe and tobacco pouch from his ulster pocket, handed the coat to Watson, and turned back to Holmes who said, "Help yourself to a cup of Mrs. Hudson's fine coffee and pull that side chair up to the fire. I want to discuss the Weatherill case."

He had taken a sip of coffee and was lighting his pipe when Holmes asked, "Do you read the agony columns, Pitt?"

"Occasionally, but not daily as you do."

"What do you make of this?" asked Holmes, handing him the newspaper. One Personal was circled and it read: **Hec—No rubba. No Brahms. Dock frog. Ship & C 21st. Last dog. P.**

"I'm not sure. *Rubba* is Cockney slang for pub, if memory serves me."

"Rhyming slang, actually," said Holmes. Rubba refers to *rub-a-dub-dub, three men in a tub*. Rhymes with pub. Brahms refers to *Brahms and Liszt*, meaning pissed or drunk. Frog is *frog and toad*, meaning road. Ship & C is the name of a pub. And of course, *Last dog* refers to the second dog-watch. Jack Poston, the man who shot MacLeish wasn't alone in the original Weatherill robbery he did time for, and I suspect his partner in the murder was the man this personal is directed to. His friend is a small time thief named Hector Bream who is given to heavy drink daily, or as often as his purse will permit. This Personal should lead to the apprehension of both men two days hence. Translated, it says, '*Hector—Stay away from pubs. Don't get drunk. Take the dock road to the Ship & Crown, a pub in Dockside, on the 21st between six and eight o'clock in the evening. Poston.*' I think if you convey this information to MacLeish, he and Inspector Bell can be waiting for them when they meet."

Pitt, pipe half way to his mouth, stared at Holmes. Watson picked up the coffee pot and refilled his cup. "Now you know how I feel, Joshua. Ten thousand readers, other than the one that ad is intended for, could read it and not understand or give it a second thought. Holmes, on the other hand…"

"I'm convinced you're correct," said Joshua, "but it begs the question of why wait two days? More importantly, perhaps, is where? The police will be combing the streets, checking places known to hide men on the run."

Holmes handed the newspaper to Pitt, took a sip of coffee, sat back reflectively and lit his pipe. "Well, it's entirely possible if the force throws their net wide, they'll discover the hideout of one or both; it's obvious they aren't together. The *personal* is proof of that. I think it unlikely, however. Until Poston's encounter with MacLeish, they didn't know they were under suspicion and took few precautions. It is conjecture, of course, but I can imagine they might hole-up in a brothel or with a woman of less than sterling moral character. It would seem to be the safest course of action for them. As to why wait two days? We can only suppose they intend to book passage on a ship to some far off destination. America, perhaps—Australia probably. You may want to consult sailing schedules for the evening of the 21st and the following day in the event their meeting plans change. They may not be apprehended at the Ship & Crown, but I think it highly probable. Having been shot by one of them, MacLeish will overreact, if anything, and might have half of Scotland Yard on hand."

Pitt lit his pipe and took several short puffs. "You are a marvel, Mr. Holmes. Had I seen the message in *The Daily Post*, it's unlikely I would have connected it to this case. Quite a neat piece of analysis."

"Nonsense, Pitt. In this case, it's no more than you or Watson could do if you would turn to the agony columns in one or more of our newspapers each day and become familiar with the various shorthands used. They are a font of information."

Joshua stood and placed his coffee cup on the table. "I'll be seeing MacLeish within the hour and will convey all this to him. If he asks, will you and John be available on the 21st to assist him?"

Holmes smiled. "I'm sure he'll need no assistance from us though he may ask you to be in attendance. In any case, Watson and I are leaving for Margate day after tomorrow and will be gone several days."

Watson handed Pitt his coat, hat and stick. "If you're free this evening and would like a game of chess, please stop by. Holmes will be out for the evening and I'd enjoy the company."

"I'd like that, John. About seven?"

"Seven would be fine."

Pitt hailed a four-wheeler, directed the cabbie to take him to St. Bart's, and settled back to enjoy his pipe. He decided to ask Mrs. Keating to add two daily papers to the Times they already received. *The Daily Post* and one of the cheaper rags would do nicely. Holmes was right. There was a wealth of information to be had in the personals columns. When they arrived at the hospital, he paid the cabbie, tapped out his pipe, and walked the long corridor to the alcove at the end. Miss Langston, head down, was writing something on a small piece of paper. As Pitt stopped in front of the desk, her head came up and she smiled while folding the paper and putting it in her apron pocket.

"Ah...Inspector MacLeish's brother."

"Most certainly, if that's still necessary." Pitt smiled back.

"I don't think so, Mr. Pitt. The Inspector is doing nicely and his doctor says unless there's some complication through the night, he may go home tomorrow. To be honest, I think the sister on duty in his ward would just as soon he went home today. He's a bit feisty."

Pitt laughed. "Calling for a pipe and a beer, I bet."

"You bet right. The pipe anyway. Seems he had one in his pocket but it was lost or misplaced as they brought him in."

She came around from behind the desk and preceded him down the hall to MacLeish's ward where she opened the door and then returned to the alcove. The

Inspector was propped up in bed with a copy of *The Times* lying across his lap. Pitt handed him the copy of the *Post* and said, "I think you may find the personals in this more interesting, particularly the one that is circled."

MacLeish took the newspaper, looked at it, then at Pitt, and then back to the personals. "Jasus! Poston! Has to be. 'E's tied in tight wi' Hector Bream. Done time together, dint they? Meetin' on the 21st at the Crown, are they? 'E'll be meetin' *me* by God! You done a fine job laddie, comin' across this."

"It wasn't me. It was Sherlock Holmes. I just came from his rooms. He pours over the agony columns in four or five newspapers daily and spotted this."

"Well, I'll be...Don' tha' take all...Bell an' me, we'll be waitin' for 'em, though I dare say I'll be keeping out o' sight. 'E knows my face for sure. Would you care to be joinin' us, laddie? If so, you may be needin' a revolver."

"I would be happy to join you and I have two pistols: an American Smith and Wesson and a Webley."

"Well, either will do nicely. I'm ta be getting' out o' here on the morrow but in the meantime, ya wouldnae happen tae 'ave a spare pipe an' tobacco would ya?"

"As so happens, I do." He reached inside his coat, pulled out the Charatan pipe and handed it to MacLeish along with his pouch of tobacco. "Here you are, Mac; you can break this one in over the next couple of days."

"Ah, laddie, Tha's your new one. I canna be takin' that."

"You most certainly can. Consider it a get well present. The sister tells me we can smoke out on the solarium. Can you make it alright?"

"Laddie, for a bowl o' tobac, I'd walk back tae Dockside." He eased out of the bed and took the pipe from Pitt. "Tis a fine pipe, laddie. Are ya sure?"

"I'm sure, Mac. That's the reason I brought it with me."

The solarium was a partially glassed in area with several meager potted plants and some small wrought iron tables and chairs scattered about. They sat for a half hour smoking and talking, till MacLeish indicated he wanted to return to the ward. As Pitt left, he paused at the door and glanced back. The Inspector had his eyes closed but was smiling and had his hands crossed on his chest over the pipe and pouch of tobacco. He promised he'd return in the morning to take the Inspector home and they would talk more then about plans for the apprehension of Poston and Bream.

He'd hoped to see Miss Langston on his way out but the alcove was empty. When he reached the front door and walked outside, he was surprised to see Fin perched on top of his hansom about thirty feet away from the steps.

"Hello Fin. How do you manage to be here?"

"Mornin' Gov. I stopped ta your rooms and your landlady said you'd likely be 'ere after seeing Mr. 'olmes. Auld Fin 'as scarffed a bit o' news he thought you might like ta hear. Would ya be likin' ta ride up top?"

Pitt climbed up next to Fin and on the way back to Baker Street, the cabbie told him that word in the pubs had Hec Bream involved in the murder of Weatherill with Poston, though it was Poston who'd done the deed. Bream had been seen in several pubs drinking heavily and seemed to have plenty of money, which was unusual. No one had seen him since late yesterday afternoon though, so he might have gone to ground somewhere. As they pulled up in front of the rooming house, Pitt handed Fin additional money, asking him to buy what information he could and if Bream's hiding place was found, to report back. If not, to pick him up at about eight o'clock the following morning.

He was just climbing the stairs to the front door when he spotted a familiar figure coming down the street, wearing the same broken down hat with wilted flower bobbing and weaving at each step. It was Molly Brick and she was waving at Pitt. He had been of assistance to Molly some time earlier when her *Mum* had gone missing and it was a case that ended both successfully and humorously.

He smiled good naturedly. "Good day, Miss Brick. Your Mum isn't missing again, is she?"

"No sor, she haint. Moved in with me, 'asn't she?"

"Well, I'm glad to hear that. How can I help you?"

"I'm thinkin' it be t'other way round, Mr. Pitt. There's a cabbie named Fin been spreadin' word you be lookin' for a bloke named Poston an' 'is mate, Bream."

"That's right, both me and the police."

"Haint havin' no truck w' coppers, unerstan, but ya done me a good turn a while back an' I can return a favor, can't I."

"Would you like to come in, Miss Brick?"

He could see she was hesitating, probably not overjoyed with the thought of climbing three flights of stairs. She was a couple of stone on the heavy side. "You look as though you've walked a ways on this damp day, and a small gin would refresh you."

The offer of gin turned the tide and she smiled. "Aye, sor, 'twould."

She settled into the chair at the side of his desk as he poured about three fingers of Bombay in a glass and handed it to her. She drank half in a gulp. "Tha's sweet, sor, it is."

"You were saying you know something about Poston and Bream?"

"Als I know of Poston is 'e shot tha' copper, dint 'e? Bream, now, been to my place for a day."

And a night too, Pitt suspected, but didn't say so. "Is he still there, and how do you know it's Bream?"

"Tol me right off, dint 'e? Says 'is name is Hec Bream. Says 'e pays in cash…'cept 'e dint. Gave me this 'ere pocket watch instead. Said it were worth five quid or more." She took a gold watch from her purse and handed it to him. "Mum said 'e left this mornin' for I rolled out but is comin' back. Leastways, 'e told Mum 'e would."

Pitt took the watch and opened it. An elegant A.W. was engraved inside the cover. It had to be Weatherill's. He snapped shut the cover and moved around to the other side of his desk where he picked up a pipe, tamped and lit it.

"I'll give you five pounds for it, Miss Brick. Did Bream tell your Mum when he'd be back?"

"If it are like yesterday, 'e'll be drinkin' till early evening, then look ta sleep. That'd be maybe two hours from now."

Damn! Hardly enough time, he thought. Aloud, he said, "Give me your address and then I want you to go home and collect your Mum. I'll give you a few extra shillings and you can take her to a pub for a bite and a drink. I'll need your key to get into your rooms."

"Got no door key. Prop chair ta door when we're there, don't I? Got a hasp lock outside if we're both leavin'."

"Alright then, leave the hasp lock unfastened and I'll be there within the hour. Do you know if Bream has a gun?"

"Dint see one but dint touch 'is pockets, did I? Mightn't surprise me though."

After asking her to describe Bream, he saw her off and then sat down to pen a short note to Inspector Bell at the Yard, giving what few particulars he had and asking the inspector to meet him at Molly's place, bringing no more than one other man. Pitt was afraid a crowd would scare off Bream. If Watson were available, Pitt would pick him up on the way. He then went into his bedroom, opened his small Simmons safe and took out an American Smith & Wesson revolver in .38 caliber leaving the large caliber Webley inside. The Smith would fit easily in his coat pocket.

He slipped on his coat and hat, put the revolver in his right pocket, pipe and tobacco pouch in his left, took up his blackthorn and headed downstairs. He found Mrs. Keating in the kitchen and handed her some shillings and the note, asking her to have her boy take it to Scotland Yard in a cab. That done, he headed down Baker Street to 221B in a mist mixed with cold rain.

Watson was in but Holmes was not. With a few minutes explanation, the good doctor was ready, and pocketed his service revolver at Pitt's suggestion. They quickly hailed a hansom and headed for Chapman Street on the edge of Whitechapel. They had gone but a short distance when Pitt heard Watson chuckle.

"Share your humor, John?"

"I was just thinking…when I opened the door and saw the expression on your face, I fully expected you to say, 'Watson, your coat! The game is afoot!' I haven't heard that for a while."

Pitt laughed. "It crossed my mind, but I am not Sherlock Holmes, and he seems to have captured that phrase as his own."

"That he has," said Watson with a smile, settling back in the corner and attempting to light his pipe while fighting the sway and bounce of the cab on the cobbles. He finally gave up. "We should be there in twenty minutes or so. How do you intend to handle this?"

"If he's already there, I'm afraid the element of surprise is lost and we'll have to wait for Inspector Bell. If he's not arrived, however, we'll prop a chair against the door as Molly does and wait for his knock. He knows they do that and shouldn't think anything amiss. It would be nice if one of us could be in the hallway and one inside but we'll have to see what its like when we arrive."

Watson turned slightly toward Pitt. "It just occurred to me, that I don't have the faintest idea what he looks like."

"Molly said he is of medium build, with brown hair and eyes, carries one shoulder lower than the other and as of this morning, unshaven. She also said he's wearing a dirty, tan docker's coat and knit wool cap. In her words, a right sorry looking cove."

"That's close enough. I doubt we'll mistake him for someone else."

Molly's rooms were one floor up in a run-down brick rooming house that smelled of curry, cabbage, and over cooked pork. Threadbare and puckered carpet was laid along the hallway as a runner but showed large snatches of wood throughout its length. The lock was open but hanging in the loop of the hasp. Pitt took his revolver out and tapped lightly at the door but when there was no answer, gave it a gentle shove and it opened readily. There was no one in the sitting room, which was pretty much a mess with woman's garments scattered throughout. He checked the bedroom but it was empty as well. It was furnished with one bed, unkempt, a dresser with mirror and a small side chair. In the sitting room there was a makeshift cot on one corner and Pitt suspected either mother or daughter slept there when the other had company. God knew what they did if they both had guests.

Watson stood just inside the front door, revolver at the ready. As Pitt re-entered the sitting room he shrugged his shoulders. "Empty. But if Molly's right, he could be returning at any time. There's a cleaning closet just across the hall and if there's room, I could stand inside and wait there. With you inside the sitting room, we'd have him trapped between us."

"It sounds reasonable, Joshua. I only hope Inspector Bell doesn't come barging in ahead of Bream, or at the same time, and spoil things."

"Nor I, but I did caution him to bring only one other Yarder with him, if that. Given the circumstance, I'm sure he'll exercise caution."

Pitt opened the door to the hallway closet, shifted a mop and bucket to one corner and then stood inside, leaning one shoulder against the inner door sill. Ten minutes went by, then fifteen. He was wondering if Bell might not make an appearance when he heard the front door open and footsteps on the stairs. Whoever it was stumbled, cursed, and then continued to the second floor. Pitt heard him shuffle down the hallway and pause at Molly's door, before he ventured a look. He saw a broad back in a tan docker's coat just starting to push at the door. Pocketing his revolver, he leaped forward but caught his foot in a raised section of carpet and fell heavily to the floor. Bream turned, drew a short bladed dirk from inside his coat, and took a step toward Pitt who was struggling to his feet.

"Bloody 'ell!" Bream took another step toward Pitt, knife hand extended slightly and slicing back and forth in a well-practiced motion.

As the hoodlum moved forward, Watson came through the door, took one step, and cracked his service revolver against the back of Bream's head who half turned before slumping to the floor. Placing his left foot on top of Bream's knife hand and his revolver against the back of his right ear, he shouted, "Don't move!" Then in a quieter voice, "You alright, Joshua?"

"I'm fine, John, thank you. Tripped on the damned carpet." Pitt stood, then bent down and removed the knife from Bream's hand. "Double edged, razor sharp, and well used from the looks of it."

Bream was unconscious, or appeared to be, and Pitt rolled him over. He had a thin scar that ran from the bridge of his nose under his left eye to mid cheek. "It would appear he's been on the receiving end of a similar knife at one time, John."

"That it would, and probably more scars where we can't see them. We'll have to find some way to tie him up till we can get him to the Yard."

At that moment, they both heard footsteps on the stairs. Seconds later, Inspector Bell, followed by a Police Constable appeared at the end of the hallway."

He nodded to Watson. "Good day, Doctor. I got your note, Mr. Pitt, 'pon my return from hospital visiting MacLeish and came quickly as I could. I take it this is Bream?"

"He fits the description," said Joshua, "and came at me with his knife before Dr. Watson ended his attack."

Bream was starting to come around and Inspector Bell turned to the constable. "Caution 'im an' put the darbys on 'im. We'll find out more when we get 'im to the station. Tis a nice piece of work 'ere gentlemen. I'll enter it in my report."

Pitt glanced at Watson, then turned to Inspector Bell. "No need for us to appear in your report, Mr. Bell. It would be just as good for you to say you made the arrest based on information received, all of which is quite true even if a few of the finer points are left out."

"Well, I thank you sirs. It will look good on my record. I'll also add that the tip came from acquaintances of Inspector MacLeish, which will reflect on 'is as well."

Watson had pocketed his revolver and was in the process of lighting his pipe. "Well Joshua, what say you to supper and a game or two of chess? I'm sure we can impose on Mrs. Hudson to provide our evening meal."

"A meal and chess should provide the perfect combination to end the day though I think one game will be sufficient. I plan to turn in early tonight."

As they left the rooming house, Pitt spotted Molly coming up the street but her *Mum* was nowhere in sight. "We've locked the door, Molly, and Bream's safely in the hands of Scotland Yard thanks to you. Is your Mum not with you?"

"Aye, well...She met this gent at the pub, now dint she?"

Pitt smiled knowingly, then took a sovereign from his pocket and pressed it into her hand. "Here's something additional for your trouble, Molly. You take care, now."

"Aye, sor, that I will, and thank you."

As she mounted the steps, he took pipe and pouch from his pocket, filled the pipe and put a match to it. After taking several short puffs, he turned to Watson. "She's a good sort, John, in spite of her occupation."

"She seems to be. Sadly, I'm sure her occupation, as you put it, is born of necessity, as is true of thousands of women in the city. It's the only commodity they have to sell for their bread and cheese."

And gin, thought Pitt, but didn't say it. They hailed a four-wheeler and returned to 221B. As it turned out, they played three games of chess, Watson winning two and Pitt winning one, before they called it a night and Pitt returned to his own rooms. It had been a long day and even the cold rain on the way back didn't counteract the several glasses of Port after supper. He was asleep within minutes.

He hadn't intended to sleep in, but slept soundly till awakened by Mrs. Keating's tap at the front room door and cheerful, "Good morning, Mr. Pitt. I think we can expect a nice day, today. The rain stopped through the night and the skies are clear, though tis still a bit cool outside. Tea and scones on the tray."

"Thank you, Mrs. Keating," was about all he could manage. His throat and mouth were parched from too much Port and too many pipes the night before. He slipped on his robe and made it to his sitting room just as the door closed behind her. He poured himself a cup of the strong Assam tea he favored, but didn't light a pipe. That could wait till his second cup. He sat at his desk sipping tea and trying to remember how many glasses of Port he'd had. Not that it mattered much. Drinking to excess was a rare occasion for him and simply remembering how he felt this morning would warn him off similar behaviors in the near future. He lit a pipe with his second cup of tea and felt better for it. The sweeter taste of Arcadia tobacco was both compliment and counterpoint to the strong tea.

The events of the previous evening came back to him and though Inspector Bell managed to take Bream from the rooming house with little fanfare, he was sure word would get out somehow. The only question was whether Jack Poston would hear of Bream's arrest before Scotland Yard had the chance to nab him at the Ship & Crown in Dockside the following day. Well, they'd learn soon enough. His immediate task was to finish his tea and scones and get ready to fetch Inspector MacLeish from hospital. He hoped Nurse Langston would be there. He was attracted to her and thought she might feel the same way toward him.

Fin and his hansom were waiting for him as he left the rooming house and was in fine fettle, softly singing some pub song as Pitt entered the cab.

"Fine day, gov'nor. Ta hospital?"

"To the hospital, Fin, and then I think to the inspector's place."

"Right ya are. We're off!"

The hansom moved off with a lurch and Pitt slid to the curbside corner of the seat before having a chance to pull is pipe from his pocket. Leaning forward, he told Fin to take his time, that they were early and not expected yet. In spite of the quick start, he smiled at the thought of Fin singing while traveling over the rough and rugged cobbles and had to admit that the first sunshine in perhaps ten days was welcome.

When they arrived at St. Bart's, he was surprised to see MacLeish standing on the steps out front talking to none other than Elizabeth Langston. When he stepped out of the hansom, Miss Langston smiled at him, but to MacLeish, she said, "I see your brother has arrived."

"Me brother?"

Pocketing his pipe, Pitt smiled and replied, "Never mind. It's a long story that I'll be happy to tell over a pint later on. Good morning, Miss Langston. It's nice to see you."

"And you, Mr. Pitt, though I suspect you'll not be visiting St. Bart's in the near future."

"Well, let's hope not under the same circumstances in any case." He didn't add that he could easily be persuaded to visit under other circumstances.

Looking directly at Pitt, she smiled and as if reading his mind, said, "If you are in the vicinity, you might stop in to say hello. If I'm free, we could have a cuppa."

"I'd like that very much. Perhaps in a day or so…"

"I'll look forward to it."

MacLeish, watching this exchange with a grin, finally spoke up. "Weel laddy, we'd best be going. I want tae visit ta Yard. Bell were here last evening an' gave me particulars of Bream's capture. Seems you and Dr. Watson took ta lead, an' a fine piece of work it was, according tae him."

"We asked Inspector Bell not to include us in his report but just to refer to the capture as the result of one of your sources."

"An' that' he did, lad, an' something else as well. 'E let it slip on the street that they'd arrested Gunner LeFarge, a Frenchy jewel thief down on his luck. No such person so far as we know, but if ta story holds for a day or two, it mightn't alert Poston. An' tha' means I'll show up for ta meeting at the pub instead o' Bream. If you'd be free tomorrow evening, lad, you might enjoy a glass at the Ship and Crown. Can't say as I recommend their food though."

Pitt opened the door to the cab and as MacLeish climbed in, said, "I'll take that as a formal invitation and come with revolver in pocket."

"Aye laddie, tha' might be wise."

The remainder of the day was uneventful. They stopped by Scotland yard for a couple of hours to meet with Inspector Bell and firm up plans for the following evening. Bell strongly suggested MacLeish keep out of sight, perhaps waiting outside the pub so as not to alert Poston immediately. Reluctantly, Mac agreed, though his desire to get his man, and to pay him back for being shot, were in equal measure. Though not as a group, Pitt, Bell, and one other inspector from the Yard would wait inside, while MacLeish and two constables would remain hidden outside. Six men seemed sufficient if they could catch Poston by surprise, though Pitt was certain that after he'd murdered one man and having attempted to murder a policeman, Poston would risk all not to be taken. It would be a dangerous game.

As they pulled up in front of his flat, MacLeish tapped the dottle from the pipe Pitt had given him in the hospital and paused at the kerb. "I have tae tell ya lad, tis as fine a pipe as I've owned an' I thank ya for it."

"You're welcome, Mac. I can see you enjoy it but it might do well with a couple of days rest in your rack. Smoke one of your old stand-bys; it will seem like an old friend. I'll see you tomorrow evening before six."

After telling Fin to pick him up at half past four the following day, he was greeted at the door by Mrs. Keating who told him dinner would be in an hour and she'd made fruit tarts to be served with cream for dessert. He told her it sounded delicious and would be down to the dining room in an hour.

He entered his sitting room, hung up his hat and coat after taking pipes and tobacco from the pockets and poured himself a stiff whiskey. There was a chill in the room and after taking a sip, he put a few lumps of coal on the grate, started a fire, filled a pipe, and rested his feet on the fender. Slowly puffing on his pipe and taking an occasional sip of whiskey, he gave thought to the several possibilities for the following day. Though he doubted Poston could be taken peaceably, he hoped that he would. Pitt had no desire to shoot someone but less desire to be shot or shot at. There were the other patrons of the pub to be considered as well and he thought it unlikely or impossible the police could reduce their numbers without warning Poston. And at that time in the evening the pub would be filled.

Well, nothing for it. What will be, will be. He was much a fatalist in that respect though he wouldn't have called himself that. A Deist by personal belief, though he'd attended the Church of Scotland with his mother as a lad, he tended to believe God wound up the celestial clock and then left man to his own devices. The warm fire and whiskey had their effect and he dozed off in the chair, only to be awakened by a tap at the door. It was Mrs. Keating carrying a tray.

"I suspected as much when you didn't come down for dinner so I fixed you a bite and a pot of tea. There's cream for the tart in the small pitcher."

"Thank you, Mrs. Keating. A wee dram of whiskey and a warm fire…I'm afraid I just nodded off. I'll bring the tray down when I've finished."

He didn't feel hungry but surprised himself once he'd tucked in. He finished the dinner and thoroughly enjoyed the tart for which the strong Assam tea was a counterpoint. Afterwards, he selected a pipe from his rack, a pipe similar to the one he'd given MacLeish but not a Charatan, filled it with a Gawith blend, and returned to the chair by the fire with the remainder of his tea. Samuel Gawith Tobaccos were located in Kendal, in the Lake District, and it had been over three months since he'd been there. Perhaps, after tomorrow evening's doings, there'd be time to take a few day's walking holiday that would include a visit to the tobacco shop. He fanaticized how nice it would be if Nurse Langston would accompany him. Ah well—dreams are made for that.

He returned the tray to Mrs. Keating, keeping the cozy covered teapot, telling her he'd bring it down with him in the morning. Returning to his sitting room, he stoked the fire and added another lump of coal. He had a comfortable life, he thought, as he relit his pipe and took a sip of the whiskey remaining in his glass. Far better than his early life as a child and several years spent at sea. His mother, God rest her soul, would be proud. His thoughts returned to Elizabeth Langston. He was attracted to her and she to him, or so he read it. His whiskey finished, he poured himself another cup of tea and picked up that morning's edition of The London Times but was soon nodding and decided it was time for bed.

He was awake betimes in the morning and through his bedroom door, heard Mrs. Keating's knock at his sitting room door, then enter with his morning tea and scones. "There's a light mist and a chill in the air this morning, Mr. Pitt, but I don't think it will last. I'll take last evening's teapot down with me."

"Good morning, Mrs. Keating, and thank you." He smiled and wondered what he'd do for a weather report if he ever moved from this flat. Well, he had no plans…He completed his toilet and sat down to his tea and scones that for some reason were particularly tasty. Afterwards, he lit a pipe, took a sip of tea, and then dressed in brown flannel trousers, loose cotton shirt and dark tweed waistcoat. Not having any appointments or obligations till later in the day, he took his time with the morning papers, paying particular attention to the agony columns. He found nothing untoward or out of the ordinary—certainly nothing that seemed remotely related to Poston or Bream and so spent the remainder of the morning reviewing his accounts and case notes.

About noon, a glance out the window told him the sun was shining and he decided to take a walk. He didn't have a destination in mind, but felt more like walking city streets than the Park. After filling one pipe, putting another and his tobacco pouch in his coat pocket, he headed out the door for Oxford Street. He hadn't intended to visit his tobacconist but once on Oxford and lost in thought, he soon found himself standing in front of the shop looking through the window. With a smile he thought, nothing for it but to go in. Pitt entered the shop and was immediately waved at by Mick, tobacconist and one of the best "pipe men" Pitt knew. He was mixing tobacco in a large porcelain crock.

"Mr. Pitt—Didn't expect to see you so soon."

"Just out for a walk and thought I'd stop by. Any new pipes?"

"No…Some of the same Comoy's and Charatan's you looked at before when you bought that smooth Charatan. As I said before, we rarely have Charatans or some of the other higher grades. They're mainly sold in their own shops but occasionally we can get a few. Still no new Petersons. How's that Charatan smoking for you?"

"I'm afraid I'll never know. I gave it to a friend."

"Ah…an expensive gift. He must be a good friend."

"He is that. Let me see that billiard shape Charatan in the case."

Mick handed him the pipe. It was a natural color and the bowl was slightly taller than normal for a billiard.

"May as well treat myself. I'll take it."

He paid for the pipe, filled his new purchase with tobacco from his pouch, lit it, and chatted with Mick for a few minutes before leaving the shop. He strolled another block east before crossing the street and turning back in the direction of Hyde Park.

Mrs. Keating was just coming out of the dining room as he entered the house. "Have you eaten, Mr. Pitt, or would you be likin' a glass of beer and a sandwich?"

"That sounds delicious. I'll take it up to my rooms. I may lie down for a nap afterwards. Would you wake me when Fin arrives?"

He did lie down after eating but was awake in less than an hour and was lighting a pipe when there was a tap at the door. It was Mrs. Keating.

"Fin is here, Mr. Pitt."

"Thank you. Tell him I'll be right down."

He went to the closet near his bookcase, took out an old canvas coat and soft cap, and slipped them on. He put two pipes and tobacco pouch in the left pocket and then went to the floor safe in his bedroom. There, he removed the Smith & Wesson revolver, checked to see it was loaded and placed it in his right coat pocket before going down the stairs and out the front door. Fin was perched atop the hansom waiting for him.

Where we off ta, Gov?"

"Ship & Crown, Dockside, but pull over about a city block away. I won't be needing you the rest of the evening but you might check with me tomorrow before starting your regular rounds."

"Right ya are, Gov."

They started off with a lurch as Pitt settled onto the seat and fished a pipe from his pocket. It was no mean task to fill a pipe while bouncing over the cobbles and weaving in and out of traffic but he managed. Within twenty minutes they were in the Dockside area and assailed by smells of raw sewage, garbage, and feces tossed into the streets that combined with the aroma of cooked cabbage and potatoes emanating from rooms above the shops that lined the street.

Pitt left the hansom and strolled toward the Crown, taking his time and looking for any sign of MacLeish. He didn't see him and hoped he wasn't inside. The Crown was typical of pubs along the wharf: long and narrow, with tables along one wall and serving counter along the other. Pitt walked to the counter, ordered a stout, and looked around the dimly lit room. He spotted Bell, who was looking his way and when he caught Pitt's eye, turned his head toward the far corner and raised his chin. Sitting there, half filled glass in front of him and puffing on a clay pipe, was a stout young lad with long brown hair poking out from under a watch cap. A Constable in plain clothes, Pitt was sure.

More than thirty minutes had gone by and Pitt was nursing his second stout when he saw Bell turn toward the rear of the pub. Poston! The fugitive moved just to the edge of the dim light and stopped, looking around. His eyes fell on Pitt but kept moving, paused at Bell for several seconds, and then moved on. He looked back toward Bell but by then, the Inspector had turned his back to him and appeared to be concentrating on his glass of beer. Poston moved to a table against the wall, hooking the arm of a prostitute as he walked past her and pulled her onto his lap as he sat down. He looked again toward Bell, frowning was if trying to place where he might have seen him before but then shrugged his shoulders. He leaned forward and said something to the woman. She nodded, got up, and walked to the counter. As she did, Pitt set his glass down and headed toward the rear of the room as if going outside to relieve himself, slipping his hand in his pocket and around his revolver as he walked.

Bell had turned round again facing Poston, and the Constable who'd been in the corner moved in the murderer's direction. Pitt was two steps beyond Poston when he heard him mutter under his breath, "Fook…Bell!" He'd finally recognized him. The inspector had drawn his revolver but there were patrons between him and Poston and he had no clear shot. Poston, meanwhile, stood, shoving his chair backwards, and pulled a Bulldog from his belt, bringing it up level with Bell. Patrons were screaming and trying to get out of the way when Pitt yelled, "Poston!" But the fugitive fired his first shot striking the prostitute, who was between him and Bell, in the middle of the back. She fell forward into the inspector and slid to the floor.

Pitt's first shot hit Poston below the right shoulder blade but instead of putting him down, Poston simply turned to level his revolver at Pitt. Three shots sounded as one: Pitt's, Poston's and the Constable's. Pitt and Poston both dropped to the floor, Poston dead or dying and Pitt with a wound to the inside of his right leg, mid thigh. The Constable kicked Poston's revolver aside and knelt beside Pitt as Bell was pulling his own shirt loose to wrap the wound.

Pitt was almost to a sitting position when the front door flew open and MacLiesh burst into the pub followed by two constables in uniform. Seeing his friend on the floor, the inspector rushed to him and bent down.

"Are ye alright, laddie?"

"Hit above the knee but it doesn't seem to be bleeding too badly. I think I owe inspector Bell a new shirt, though."

"I 'ave a coach outside. We'll be getting' ya ta Bart's. Bell, can you and the lads see ta this, then?"

Pitt winced. "Hurts like hell." Then nodding toward Poston as MacLeish helped him to his feet, he asked, "Is he dead?"

The constable in plain clothes nodded. "Aye, or close. Two in back and one in front. The woman's dead too."

Pitt was beginning to feel lightheaded and as his knees gave way, one of the uniformed officers caught him. They got him into the police coach and the last thing he remembered before slipping into a grey twilight was MacLeish yelling at the driver, "St. Barts—Now!"

The first thing he became aware of was the sound of soft snoring and wondered if it was his own. He opened his eyes and tried to make out where he was. The room was dim with the gaslight near the door turned down and he turned his head in the direction of the snoring. Inspector MacLiesh was asleep in a chair about three feet from the bed. Then he remembered. He remembered the encounter at the Ship & Crown, firing his revolver at Poston, and being shot himself. It was when he remembered being shot that the pain seemed to flood into his leg from hip to knee and he moaned softly.

MacLeish awoke with a start. "Are ya wi' us, laddie?"

"I think so. Is my leg with me?"

"Aye, tis that, but ta bullet creased your thigh bone and stopped under ta skin at ta back o' your leg. Yon doctor says you'll mend quickly. 'E also said a wee bit higher an' you'd be singing a different tune. On a higher note, anyway."

Pitt laughed and it brought another moan. "Hurts...Poston?"

"Dead. An' speakin' of singin' we can't shut Bream up. Once he found out Poston 'ad been killed at the Crown, 'e blamed 'im for everythin' includin' Weatherill's murder. Claims Poston did it alone. Nowt matters what 'e says. Spect 'e'll swing."

"I'd love a hot cuppa and a pipe."

"A cuppa, I can arrange, but ta pipe will hafta wait till ya can go outside to yon porch. Same rules as for me, lad. I'll see tae cuppa. Or I'll ask tha' pretty sister you know to bring some. She's been here all night, hasn't she?" And with that comment, he walked out of the room.

Pitt lay there thinking how, for him, this whole adventure had opened just several short days ago with a note handed him by a small lad asking if he'd look into the Weatherill matter—to provide whatever assistance he could to MacLeish. So much had transpired. Three men and a woman shot. A man and woman dead. When he got home to his lodgings, he'd write this case up, probably with some reference to Holmes. After all, it had begun with him, though in a sense, Dr. Watson had a leading role.

He had almost drifted off when the door opened and Elizabeth Langston entered with teapot and covered dish on a tray.

"I thought you might like some biscuits and cheese with your tea."

"That's very kind of you, but what are you doing here at this hour?"

She sat the tray on the bedside table. "What o'clock do you think it is?"

"Midnight, maybe a bit later."

"More like six in the morning and I'll be going on duty in an hour."

"MacLeish told me you were here all night."

She blushed. "Well...I was concerned and I assisted the doctor. Drink your tea now and I'll be back later to check your dressing and see if it needs changed."

Knowing he was naked under the sheet from the waist down, he stumbled trying to find a reply, then said, "Oh I don't think that will be necessary...I might find it embarrassing."

She smiled, reached out and gently touched his cheek. "Somehow, I doubt that."

END

THE KENDAL AFFAIR

There was almost no wind as large snowflakes fell softly on London, glistening in the glow of gas lamps and adding to the several inches that had accumulated during the evening. The air was crisp and pleasant, just a few degrees below freezing, as Joshua Pitt walked toward his flat on Baker Street.

It had been a delightful evening of dinner, a glass or two of Port, and a game of chess with Dr. John Watson whilst enjoying several bowls of tobacco. It was the tobacco that prompted Joshua to recall the particulars of a case that had taken him to the village of Kendal, in the Lake District, and home of Samuel Gawith tobacco blenders. Watson had just that day received a one-pound block of Brown Flake from Gawith and as a change of pace from their usual Arcadia blend, they had smoked some of the tobacco that evening.

Joshua took a sip of Port and was puffing on his pipe as he studied the board and Watson's last move. "This is a fine tobacco, John. It's been some time since I've smoked a Gawith tobacco."

"That it is. I prefer it to all other blends except Arcadia. Rich tasting, light, nutty aroma, and blended the same way for most of one hundred years. A damn sight better than that black shag of Holmes' I can tell you." They both laughed and Watson continued, "Weren't you recently in Kendal?"

"I was just thinking of that. What began as a pleasant holiday, albeit a working one, ended with my earning the enmity of an Irish nobleman, though I must admit it was well worth it. I gave him a thrashing with his own blackthorn."

"By Jove, thrashing an Irish nobleman you say? You certainly were tempting fate, Joshua. Why don't you tell me about it while we're playing? It might just distract you enough to give me an easy win."

Pitt leaned back in his chair, drew slowly on his pipe savoring the taste of the tobacco, and reflected for a moment. "It was early October, a blustery day but with sunshine, and I'd just finished making some entries in my account books when there was a knock at my sitting room door…

"I bade the visitor enter, and in walked a tall, stout, middle-aged man in tweeds. His was a florid face surrounded by whiskers known as muttonchops and a nose that was more likely red from steady drink than the cold. He strode across the floor to my desk in a brusque manner that presumed command, or at the very least, as one who is used to having his wishes or orders carried out. The moment he spoke, his brogue, though cultured, gave him away. He was certainly Irish."

"You would be Mr. Pitt?"

"I am he."

"You have been recommended by a friend of a friend. I am Sir Edwin McNee of Belfast. Perhaps you have heard of me. We raise horses, several of which have found their way to Her Majesty's stables."

"I'm afraid I haven't…"

"Well, no matter, no matter. A person of your…well, again, no matter. I have lost two items of some importance and I want you to find them: my blackthorn walking stick and my wife. I have reason to believe they are together and in England. Cumbria, the Lake District, I should think…But I'm not certain. I have neither the time nor inclination to spend flogging around the countryside searching for her but I want to recover my blackthorn. I would like you to begin immediately and I'm willing to pay your fee and all expenses for ten days for you to conduct a search for my wife. So far as anyone should know, you're on holiday, and in the event you should find her, do not approach her, but simply telegraph me. In addition, if you do locate her, I'll pay you a bonus of one hundred pounds."

"That's a generous offer, Mr. McNee, and one I should like to accept, but I'm afraid it will be at least a week before I can undertake your case. I'm currently engaged in a serious matter and it will be at least that long…"

"A week is not satisfactory, though I do understand you may have other obligations. Can you make it three days?"

"I suppose I could make some arrangements…"

"Fine, fine. I shall expect you on your way in three days then, and some communication as to where you'll be staying, or at least where you can be reached. I shall also expect contact every three days, even if you have nothing to report. A telegram will be sufficient."

And with that, he placed an envelope on my desk, turned abruptly, and walked out, not bothering to close the door.

"Well, bloody 'ell," I mumbled, using a favorite phrase of Fin, my oft-times cabbie and informant. I got up, closed the door, and returned to my desk, stopping at the sideboard to pick up a pipe and jar of tobacco. I filled the pipe, lit it, and turned to the envelope. Inside were a cheque, two photos—tintypes both—and a slip of paper. The cheque was generous, certainly enough to cover expenses for ten days of first class travel and accommodations. The first photo was of *himself* holding the blackthorn forward to the camera as if to show it off. It was a stout cudgel of about an inch and a half in diameter stem to stern, with a good three-inch knob at the top and at least thirty-five inches in length. The second photo was of his wife—at least I assumed it was his wife because at the bottom of the photo was written in ink, *Eileen McNee*. She was a very attractive Irish lass at least ten years junior to her husband. The note was quite short and read: *The shillelagh belonged to my great grandfather and was taken by wife, Eileen, for reasons that concern no one other than myself. I want it back. I will have her back as well. Your task is to find them and report their whereabouts to me. I will resolve the issue at that point. She has friends in both Kendal and Whitehaven and either city might be used as a starting point. Mrs. McNee stands slightly over five feet tall, has dark brown hair and hazel eyes. Pictures of both are enclosed. ...McNee*
PS: *Her friend in Kendal is Miss Fiona Baines, and in Whitehaven the Harold Keen family.*

Well now, I thought...well now...keeping my feelings out of this case wasn't going to be easy. I had taken an immediate dislike to Mr. McNee, his brusque and demeaning manner, and assumed he treated all around him in the same fashion, including his wife. Then again, I didn't pick and choose my employers; they chose me. And as long as I wasn't being asked to do something patently illegal, I would take their money and give them my best.

Three days later found me at Euston Station with travel bag, fishing gear, and a ticket to Oxenholm, near Kendal. I considered beginning my search in Whitehaven along the coast and at the westernmost edge of Cumbria but rejected it after receiving a response to a wire sent to Stanley Bratt, a solicitor's clerk and occasional investigator. Stanley was a long time friend from my early days in London and I had sent a telegram asking if the Harold Keen family had a young woman visitor staying with them. His reply was that the Keen family was on holiday in France and had been for three weeks.

In any case, Kendal was closer to London and therefore closer to myself, and secondly, it was also closer to Heysham, the port where the ferry from Belfast would put in after a layover in Douglas on the Isle of Man. In addition, I knew the city of Kendal and had a distant relative there, whereas I was unfamiliar with Whitehaven. So Kendal it was. I won't deny that subconsciously, the fact that Samuel Gawith Tobaccos were located there might have played some part in the decision, but at the time, I didn't think of it.

The trip was uneventful, pleasurable in fact, since I had a compartment to myself compliments of my employer. I enjoyed tea and cakes, and a couple of bowls of tobacco while watching the countryside unfold as we moved northwest from London. About an hour into my trip, the sun began to peek through broken clouds with the promise of a fine day by journey's end and I caught myself dozing in the warmth that streamed in through the carriage car window. I woke to the sound of the sliding door to my compartment and the Conductor leaning in to tell me we'd be arriving in Oxenholm in five minutes. I thanked him, got my bags down from the overhead rack and lit a pipe. From Oxenholm, less than two miles from Kendal, I could connect to a local train or hire a trap or hansom. Since the difference was only a few shillings, I would hire horse drawn if available. Not that cost was a factor; it had just become too fine a day to remain inside a train.

A trap was available and I loaded my bags behind the seat and climbed up next to the driver, giving him instructions to take me to the Riverside Inn at the south end of Kendal. It was a small inn with only fourteen rooms, but next to the River Kent and afforded easy access to some fine fly fishing, which, in keeping with my assignment, I intended to do.

The market town of Kendal lies at the eastern edge of Cumbria on the River Kent and is built largely of grey stone, earning it the nom de plume of *auld grey town*. Though it's primary source of wealth is from the wool trade, it is well known to pipe smokers for the Samuel Gawith tobacco firm and their fine blends. There is a castle once owned by the Parr family overlooking the town, and although in ruins by the end of the 16th century, it is noted for Catherine Parr, last wife of Henry VIII. At the moment, however, I was not interested in history or wool, though if I found some time, and I was certain I would, I'd visit Gawith tobaccos.

We soon arrived at the inn and after depositing my bags in my room and sending a telegram to McNee to let him know where I was staying, I struck out to visit Hamish MacLeod. He had been a friend of my parents when they were living, a distant cousin to my father, and had moved to England some thirty years before. Hamish raised sheep for many years on a farm several miles outside Kendal, but had moved to a small flat in town after his wife died and rented his farm to a nephew. I had sent a telegram to him the day before and his prepaid reply was short, in keeping with the spare nature of MacLeod: "Ta home as usual. Welcome. Hamish".

I was greeted with a smile, a warm handshake, and an immediate offer of a wee dram, which I quickly accepted. The cottage was an old one with small living quarters and somewhat crowded but cozy living room. We settled in wingback chairs near the smoke darkened fireplace which was prepared but not burning, both of us pulling pipes from our pockets in chorus as if it were planned that way. My pipe lit, I took a sip of the whisky, a fine single malt from the Highlands. After a few puffs on his pipe, Hamish leaned forward and set it in an ashtray on the step in front of the fireplace.

"So, laddie, what brings you to Kendal?"

"I hope to get a bit of fishing in, but my primary reason is to look for someone, a woman, and if I find her, report back to my employer. She's the wife of Sir Edwin McNee of Belfast and he seems to think she may be staying with friends in Kendal." I paused for a moment, drew on my pipe, then went on, suppressing a grin. "Strange as it may be, it's his blackthorn that McNee is most interested in. Seems the lady took it with her when she left."

"Ah...tis one of *those* holidays, is it? There's nowt but a bit o' domestic discord to spark the urge for travel. Mrs. McNee will be staying with friends here, then?"

"If my information is correct, it's possible she's staying with Miss Fiona Baines if she is here in Kendal, though it's almost as likely she's in Whitehaven."

Hamish rose, went to the sideboard, picked up the decanter of whisky and returned to the fireplace, pausing to refill our glasses before depositing the decanter on the hearth-step. "And when you've discovered their whereabouts, are ye to return both stick and wife to McNee?"

"No, I am not. Sir Edwin has asked that I don't approach her but simply report immediately to him by telegram. I assume he will come fetch her."

"Ye are not to make her acquaintance at all, then?"

"That is what I have been charged with, Hamish, and paid for, I might add."

"Just notify the lord and master so he can come carry her back to Ireland and beat her again with that cudgel of his."

I turned sharply toward him. "How do you know that?"

"Arthur Baines is land agent here, and a friend. For most on a fortnight, his daughter has been seen aboot with a lady who is obviously visiting, though I've nowt seen her aboot lately. I met them on market day soon after she arrived, but I was no formally introduced, and she held back behind Fiona as though shy. She was wearing a thin veil, but it didn't hide one bruise on her cheek and another near her left eye. Nor did the long sleeves of her dress hide the bruises on both wrists. She's a small slip of a lass w' long, dark hair and a pert manner about her, but she has been ill treated, lad. Money or no, I'd no be inclined to inform on the lass to the rotten blighter that beat her…if tis the lady you're looking for."

I sat there for a couple of minutes, puffing on my pipe, thinking over what he had said, finally arriving at a the only conclusion my conscience would allow. I took a sip of my whisky and turned to Hamish. "Can you arrange an introduction?"

He smiled. "I thought you were no to meet with the lady."

"Dammit, Hamish, can you arrange for me to meet her!"

"Aye, I can, if she's still here. As I said, I've no seen her lately."

"Please try. And if it is Eileen McNee, do not speak a word of my reason for being here. I will broach the subject myself to her when we meet, if I think it prudent. I have only met Sir Edwin on one occasion but my impression is he is just the sort to beat a wife, or dog, or servant who did not follow his wishes. Perhaps we can do something about that."

"Aye, an' mayhap crossing the rich an' powerful will earn you a clew bag full of trouble as well."

"I've seen trouble before, Hamish."

He cocked an eye at me, picked up his pipe, and said, "I'll bet you have, me lad, I'll bet you have…"

I was up betimes the following morning and fished until almost ten o'clock, catching several nice trout but only keeping one to have as dinner that evening. The hotel cook assured me she would turn out a fine curried rice with it and had an apple tart and cream on hand for dessert. I had repaired to my room and was enjoying a strong cup of tea with a pipe when there was a light tap at my door. It was a young lad of about ten in knickers, tweed cap and jacket.

"Mr. Pitt?"

"Yes."

"From Mr. MacLeod," he said, as he handed me an envelope.

I reached in my trouser pocket for some change but he was turning away.

"Been paid, sir."

"Well, thank you."

"Welcome, I'm sure."

The note was short and read: *If evening fishing does not attract your attention, come to my place at seven o'clock and we will walk to the Baines residence together. Hamish.*

Well, now…a stroke of luck? Perhaps, but it was entirely possible this woman who was visiting the Baines was not Mrs. McNee. I thought it unlikely—the description Hamish gave was close to what I expected. If it was her, I would be compromising one of the instructions given me by Edwin McNee, namely not to approach her but to simply contact him, but after talking with Hamish, I had made up my mind to see this woman first hand anyway. That did bring to mind two questions: why should I not approach her; what reason could McNee have for not wanting me to make his wife's acquaintance? And beyond that, how was I to confirm her identity without some contact? I thought this over and decided I would make such determinations as necessary on my own hook. My imagination by this time was racing. I pictured her fleeing Ireland after a beating with the blackthorn by a drunken McNee. Fleeing with blackthorn in hand, to friends in England who would shelter her. After a few moments of this, and a return to reality, I had to admit the woman could have sustained the injuries falling from a horse and in fact, she may not be Eileen McNee at all. Well, blast it, I would find out that evening. In the meantime and since I was at my leisure, an afternoon nap before my trout dinner was in order.

Hamish was standing in his open doorway, smoking a pipe, when I approached his cottage. The delightful scent of his tobacco carried to me on the breeze as I walked up the narrow path.

"Fine aroma, Hamish. What are you smoking?"

"Some of Sam Gawith's Best Brown. Would you like some?"

"That I would. I want to get to his shop, and should have walked there this afternoon, but was lazy and took a nap instead."

We walked inside and Hamish proffered an old porcelain humidor of sliced tobacco to me. I took a large bent Peterson from my pocket, crumbled some of the tobac, and filled my pipe. Whilst I was doing this, Hamish took several of the slices, wrapped them in a small square of heavy paper and handed it to me. "For later," he said with a smile, "and in case you don't make it to Gawith's tomorrow, as well."

I pocketed the tobacco and thanked him while he turned down the gaslight on the whitewashed stone wall near the fireplace. We walked out the door and as he turned to pull it closed, he said, "You may like to know I saw Arthur Baines in town this afternoon and your missing lady is in fact staying with them. I gave nothing away. I simply mentioned I'd seen his daughter and a woman who I didn't know while doing some marketing. He volunteered that it was Eileen McNee, a close friend of his daughters. Kind of creates an ethical dilemma for you, doesn't it?"

"Is that an evil grin I see on your face, you old Highland bastard?"

Hamish laughed aloud. "That it is laddie, that it is."

It was but a short, pleasant, ten minute walk to the Baines residence; a large stone dwelling of two stories in the shape of a T with Tudor chimneys, situated on several acres of well groomed estate. An Elm flanked lane curved up to a cobblestone area directly in front of the entrance that was wide enough to accommodate several carriages.

"Mr. Baines must be a prosperous man," said I.

"Aye…weel, in addition to being land agent, he's in the whiskey trade—much of it single malt. Owns two warehouses."

We both pocketed our pipes as we walked up the steps to the front door and Hamish gave the bell knob a twist. Within a few seconds the door was opened by a short, stout, full bearded fellow in dark trousers and starched shirt.

Hamish smiled. "Good evening, Jameson, I believe Mr. Baines is expecting us."

"Yes sir, he is. He's in his office."

We followed the butler down a hallway that was wide, grey marble tiled, and from all appearances ran the depth of the house to a large open alcove showing stairs that ran off both side to the upper floor. Half-way down the hallway, Jameson paused, opened a door for us and stood to one side.

Arthur Baines was sitting behind a huge desk, one of the largest I'd ever seen, and it immediately occurred to me that it may have been built in the room, for I could see no doorway that would admit it. Baines himself, was a large man with salt and pepper hair and beard, and as he stood to come round the desk to greet us, I realized he was at least six feet tall and must have gone fifteen stone and perhaps more.

"Hamish, good to see you. And this is the young lad visiting you, I take it?"

"Aye, well…he's staying at the Inn on the river. Closer to fishing than my place." Hamish made introductions.

"It's a bit chilly. Have you had any luck yet, Lad?"

"I had a trout dinner this evening," I answered, shaking hands. The man had a firm grip, but not crushing—just assertive.

"Capital, capital…Would you care for a drop of whiskey?"

Without waiting for an answer, Baines went to a tall cabinet on the wall behind his desk, selected a decanter from the several that stood there and poured a generous amount into three glasses. As he handed ours to us he said, "There are cigars in the humidor on the desk if you would care for one."

I took my Peterson from my pocket. "I think I'll stay with my pipe."

"Fine, fine…as you can see by the rack on my desk, I smoke both pipe and cigar but enjoy a cigar more with my whiskey I think."

Led by Baines, we walked to the far side of the room where several chairs and side tables were gathered in a setting in front of a burning fireplace. As an office, the room was misleading. It was far more library than office, with floor to ceiling bookshelves on two walls and ladders on rails to reach the top shelves. Several books sat on the tables and an open copy of the Strand Magazine lay on the floor near the chair chosen by Baines. After sitting, I leaned forward and glanced down at it. He saw me and chuckled. "Another Holmes exploit by Dr. Watson, I'm afraid. I seem to be addicted to them and will often read them more than once."

"I live little more than a city block from them," said I, "and occasionally play chess with John when we're both free."

"And what is your profession, Mr. Pitt?"

"Joshua, please, or simply Pitt. I'm a private inquiry agent and have a small but successful practice in London that keeps me interested and occupied. I'm certainly not in the same league as Sherlock Holmes though I have been honored to provide some small assistance to him on several occasions. He is certainly *the* genius in his field."

Arthur Baines looked at me for a few seconds, then said, "I take it you're here on holiday then, and not on business."

Though the question was not altogether unexpected, I was not certain I wanted to give myself away just yet. I could see Hamish looking at me with a hint of a smile on his face, knowing full well I was doing some mental squirming. "I'll admit I left London partly for business reasons but it was the fishing that brought me to Kendal and I hope to make the most of it while here."

"Hmmm…there was an agent here a couple of weeks ago, a rather crude and vulgar chap, looking for someone we know but weren't prepared to discuss. He met with no success and went elsewhere. He was a small, ferret-faced bloke named Wingate, and I'm afraid I spoke a bit harshly to him when he approached me with questions. He left the following day."

I tried to hide my surprise though the look on my face, I'm sure, gave me away. So McNee had Wingate on the case and he had failed, or at least moved on to other locations. I suspected the former. I knew Wingate, or at least knew of him. To call him an unethical bastard would be treating him lightly. I also suspected that when Baines said he spoke harshly to Wingate, he was understating his case. Wingate, when confronted with a mountain of a man like Baines, would have quickly left for less threatening climes and reported to McNee that his wife couldn't be found. I had a decision to make. I made it.

"Mr. Baines, I'd like you to hear me out..." He glanced at Hamish, who nodded affirmatively. I began at the beginning with McNee's visit to my office, my immediate dislike of him and growing distaste for the task I was assigned. I finished with the comment that I suspected Mrs. McNee had been severely ill treated by her husband and my objectives in this matter had taken an opposite turn. If what I surmised was correct, then nothing would suit me better that to somehow turn the tables on McNee. When I finished, I took a sip of my whiskey and relit my pipe.

Baines stared pensively at the fire for a moment before he spoke. Finally, he sat his cigar in an ashtray and turned to me. "Your suppositions are correct, Joshua. When Eileen McNee came here she was beaten so badly I'm at a loss to explain how she could have traveled. She is of the same age as my daughter Mary, and they met several years ago while attending boarding school near Belfast. Three weeks ago, she wired Mary that she was ill and coming to Cumbria but it was only when she arrived that we realized what her *illness* was. She has, for all practical purposes, been hiding here, though occasionally she's been out and about with my daughter. We cannot, in good conscience, return her to her husband, but are at a loss as to a solution. English law, being what it is as regards married women, leaves much to be desired, and in fact we are in some jeopardy for harboring her. If you can offer some solution, Joshua, I would certainly entertain it."

"I do have an idea but it may involve confrontation with McNee, and I must think it through before I propose it. In the meantime, would it be possible for me to meet the lady? I have been forming opinions at a distance, as it were, and would like to see and speak with her first hand. I think we must find out what her intentions are before I act. After all, if she simply intends to go back to him regardless, then there is little I can do, or should do, as distasteful as I may find it." I finished my whiskey, tapped the remaining ash out of my pipe and waited for Baines to speak, but it was Hamish we heard from first.

"Weel laddie, as I see it, if the lady did suffer a severe thrashing at the hands of her husband, there's nowt she or you can do inside the law. That leaves you two options: one, get McNee here on the pretext that his wife has been spotted, that you know where she is, and confront the bastard when he arrives. Or...fish for five days and wire him that his wife is nowhere to be found. Shrug your shoulders, spit, and walk on, as it were. Knowing what little I know of you, however, the second is probably not an option you would easily abide by."

I started to reply but Arthur Baines leaned forward and interrupted. "There are several things…I can arrange for you to meet Mrs. McNee and will do so in a few minutes, but I would urge you to speak truthfully with her and tell her your purpose for being here. If you tell her you have been charged only with finding her and reporting back to her husband, it will become immediately obvious to her that you have disregarded your employer's instructions and wish to help. She is a bright, well educated woman and will understand that. I do have a concern, however, and it is a personal one. As much as I'd like to hand out a thrashing to McNee myself, or at the least, observe it, I would much prefer that no confrontation occur here at my home. It may seem mercenary to you but I have business interests that could suffer as a result and that would impact on my family."

Typical of pipe smokers, I took advantage of refilling my pipe with some of the tobacco Hamish had given me while I thought through what had been said. "Hamish is right; I cannot just walk away. On the other hand, and however unlikely it may turn out to be, I would prefer to reach some resolution with a touch of finesse as opposed to physical conflict. McNee, however, strikes me as one who would listen more to the whip than the word and it may come to that. I would hope not, but it may." I paused to light my pipe and as I did, Baines rose, walked to the sideboard and returned with the whiskey decanter to refill our glasses. After taking several short puffs on my pipe, I went on. "As you say, though, the decision to take any action rests with Mrs. McNee and that can probably be decided in short order when I talk with her."

Baines set his glass on the table and stood. "I believe she's in the garden with my daughter. I'll ask them to step in."

He was gone but a few moments and returned with two strikingly attractive young women in tow. He made introductions, though it was obvious from the first which was Mrs. McNee. She had made no attempt to hide the yellow blemish under one eye and her attitude was one of reticence. She did not proffer her hand and merely nodded when Mr. Baines spoke her name. It was when he added that I was an inquiry agent from London that her head came up sharply and she looked first at him and then myself. As if not noticing, Baines went on, "Mr. Pitt is here, Eileen, because he has been employed by your husband to find you. He has not compromised you, however, and it would be in your best interests to talk with him. I think if you sat by the fireplace, you would be comfortable. Would you like a sherry?"

She paled and appeared ready to faint. Pocketing my pipe, I reached out and took her arm. "Please, Mrs. McNee, I only wish to help you. Come over and sit near the fire and hear me out."

Haltingly, she came with me and took a seat as Baines poured a small sherry and handed it to her. She sipped, placed the glass on the table and turned to me, saying in a more forceful voice that surprised me, "You cannot help, Mr. Pitt. If Edwin finds me, he will drag me back to Ireland to repeated beatings when he is drunk or if I do not favor him. There is nothing you can do, or English law will provide, that will prevent that."

There was fire in this woman; I could see that, but it was a fire suppressed by fear. She was handsome...nay, she was attractive with both an inward and outward beauty and I have to admit I was quite taken with her. She struck me as one who would be as much partner as wife—a woman equal to a man and one who, given the opportunity, would take adversity head on. I couldn't help but think, "If things were different..."

I pulled my pipe from my pocket and tamped the ash before lighting. "Mrs. McNee, though it may seem unlikely, there may be some way to reach an accommodation with your husband and I am willing to try, but I must first have more information than I have. Will you answer some questions?"

"Accommodation is not in my husband's vocabulary, but yes, if I can."

"How long have you been married?"

"Three years this past August. I was twenty at the time."

"Some of these questions may seem impertinent, but that is not my intention. I only seek to form a complete picture if I am to intervene. Mr. McNee seems quite a bit older that you. How is it that the marriage came about?"

"You mean did I love him, or fall in love with him? Well...yes and no. Our meeting was arranged by well meaning members of both families, though I dare say there was more at stake than my future happiness. My family lives on a small freehold of about ten hectares that borders his estate. We raise sheep for wool and some vegetables for our own use and some to sell in the city. I suppose you would call us middleclass. I was told that Mr. McNee had seen me at a distance on several occasions while I was on holiday from school and wished an introduction. This was made known to my parents and it was arranged. Though it was never spoken of to me, I suspect there may have been benefits of a match mentioned to my father because soon after our betrothal, he purchased additional land from Mr. McNee. Edwin introduced me to parties, dances, and a class of people, the likes of which I'd never seen before. He drank too freely even then, but he was a gentleman in every way and I thought little of it. I was never certain that I loved him but believed I might in time, and a better match was unlikely for me. We were married in August, 1892."

"And when was the first time he became physically abusive to you?"

"Almost a year to the day we were married. He'd been drinking and wanted me to accompany him into the city. I told him no and without a word of warning he struck me twice with his open hand. They were vicious blows that knocked me to the floor and I was faint for minutes afterward. He left without saying a word. There were several other occasions but in the past six months they became more frequent and he took to using that blackthorn he has, the cudgel that has been in the McNee family for generations and he is rarely without. The last time was about three weeks ago and he beat me near senseless with it while I was in the garden. I must have lain there for an hour until the chamber-maid, Molly, found me and took me to the kitchen. She kept saying over and over, "You have to leave, missy, you have to get away, else he will kill you." The following day he had guests and they spent the day shooting in the fields. I packed a bag, took all the household funds from the cashbox and was on my way out the door to a waiting carriage when I spied his blackthorn in the umbrella stand. I took it as well."

I smiled. "When he came to see me, his concern seem to be more for his Shillelagh than for you."

With more grimace than smile, she said, "I'm not surprised. It was rarely out of his hand unless we had guests." The fire came back to her eyes and a grin spread across her face. "But he is without it now, is he not?"

I laughed aloud. "It would seem so. Tell me, why did you not go to your parent's home?"

"I thought of it but I wanted no trouble to fall upon their heads, and I assumed that would be the first place he would search for me when he discovered I had gone missing. Once he realized I had taken his precious blackthorn, he would be in a fury. From Belfast, I wired Mary that I would be coming to visit and day later, caught a packet to England."

"I'll be honest with you, Mrs. McNee, this situation presents almost as many problems for me as for you. I was instructed by my employer, your husband, to find you and report your whereabouts, but he specifically said not to make contact with you. As you can see, that part of the bargain has already been abridged. In addition, I make an effort not to become involved personally with the cases I take on, though admittedly, I am not always successful. This seems to be just such a case. Now we both know you have very little standing in this matter under British law and if your husband wants to drag you back to his home under restraint, he may do so legally. Divorce is always possible of course, if he will accede. My impression of him, however, leads me to believe that he would not agree to divorce, or even legal separation, unless coerced. All this is conjecture on my part, but still it begs the question, do you want to return to him, and if so, under what circumstances?"

She didn't respond immediately, but stared into the fire. Her hair glowed with highlights created by the dancing flames and I wanted to reach out and touch it; to reach out and touch her, to somehow comfort her. In spite of my feeling, I did not. Instead, I maintained my silence, stared into the fire, and smoked my pipe. Perhaps five minutes went by before she raised her head and turned to me.

"This has become a very complicated matter, Mr. Pitt, one that I have tried to ignore for several weeks. As much as I wish not to, I'm afraid I must make some decisions and I have you to thank. That is not meant in a disparaging manner. To the contrary, and to your credit, your words have forced an issue long overdue. I cannot and will not return to the life I was living under his roof. Rather I would be dead than suffer another brutal beating at his hands. But if he discovers my whereabouts and I refuse to return with him, he may take some action against my family. He is a powerful landowner with great influence and few scruples. I cannot imagine he would hesitate to exact some sort of revenge. So, Mr. Pitt, advise me. What should I do?"

It was my turn to think and I did so, taking short puffs on my pipe as was my wont while considering a thorny problem. Finally, I asked, "If circumstances were such that you could return, but without fear of violence, would you do that?"

Her answer was immediate. "No! Not only do I loath the man, but what kind of life would it be? He would take me when the mood was upon him and my opinion of myself would be no more than of a common trollop. I don't know who I would hate more—him or me."

I set my pipe on the table and took a sip of whiskey. "Do you know anything of his business dealings, anything at all that we might use threat of, to bend him in the direction of divorce?"

"No, I've never been privy to his business ventures, though I any case, there seems to be only two areas of interest for him: breeding horses and the stock markets. He seems to do exceedingly well at both. He occasionally has late night meetings with several men who speculate on a large scale. At least I get that impression from snatches of conversation overheard once before I retired for the night. Though I was not introduced, nor do I know them, I took an immediate dislike to two of his most recent visitors." She smiled. "I call one Mr. Rat and the other Mr. Weasel because that is what they remind me of. Both are slim and small with pinched faces and wary eyes that seem to dart hither and yon as if fearful of discovery."

"Do you know their names?"

"Only one. Mr. Rat. His name is Nicholas Grimes. The other's given name is Toby, I think. At least I believe that was the name I heard."

My grin gave me away. I knew them both, or at least knew of them, and she saw the expression on my face.

"Do you know them, then?"

"Oh yes. At least know of them. Nicholas Grimes and Tobias Bellows. They're well known in London for spiking the markets with rumor and then cashing in before truth is discovered and there's a downhill run on the stocks. There have been several attempts to catch them in the act but all have failed. They create the bubble and sell before it bursts."

"Bubble? Bursts?"

"They buy a cheap but respectable stock in a goldmine, for instance. Several weeks later, with help from associates, no doubt, they start a rumor that recent geological reports indicate an immanent strike of a new and promising vein. It is denied by the mining company, but no one will believe them and the stock rises. When the value of the stock reaches a level predetermined by Grimes and Bellows, they sell at what is usually an enormous profit. Soon afterwards, other speculators learn the mining company was telling the truth and the stock collapses. The rumors begun by those two cannot be traced back to them and in any case the market is always volatile and unpredictable. But people like Grimes and Bellows need backers to buy up sufficient stock in the first place because to buy in their own names would give them away. It is entirely possible your husband is one of those. If so, we may have a lever…"

"How so?"

"An implied threat often carries more weight that a real one. If I or someone else were to threaten to expose your husband's dealings with those two, the threat of exposure alone may be all we need. That same threat would also keep him from taking any action against your family."

I had risen while speaking and was standing at the fireplace with one arm leaning on the mantle. She rose and came toward me, stopping but a foot or so away, close enough that I could smell the scent of Gardenia.

"Mr. Pitt, I could kiss you."

"Mrs. McNee, I would let you." And with that, she went on tiptoe and kissed me on the cheek. I'm afraid I blushed beneath my beard but hoped it didn't show, and for once in my life, was at a loss for words. "Hmmm…yes…well…"

Hamish laughed and though I glared at him, I realized quickly that anything said further by myself would increase my embarrassment, and so wisely put my pipe in my mouth and said nothing.

Arthur Baines came forward, smiling as he filled a pipe from a floppy old leather pouch. "So, you may be able to assist Eileen? Have you a plan, then?"

"I have the makings of one but it lacks detail for the moment. I will need to send some telegrams on the morrow but I think we shall be ready two days hence. It needs getting Mr. McNee to Kendal but there should be no difficulty there. Mr. Baines, you have experience drawing up business contracts, do you not?"

"I do, certainly, but always have them reviewed by a solicitor before signing. Why do you ask?"

"I would like a document prepared for Edwin McNee's signature that will permit Mrs. McNee to petition for divorce on agreeable terms. It needs not be highly detailed but must be binding. Will you do that?"

"Of course. I will make out a draft this evening and take it to my solicitor first thing in the morning. Would you like to then see it?"

"I bow to your experience in an area where I have none, but still, I think I would."

"Fine. Come by in the morning at about nine o'clock and I will have it ready."

We enjoyed a few more minutes of light conversation before Hamish and I took our leave. He was unusually quiet but nearing his cottage, he stopped to light his pipe and in the flair of the match I could see a smile on his face. Over the bowl he said, "Weel, laddie, it would appear you have put ethics ahead of fishing, though I daresay the fact that Eileen McNee is such a pretty lass may have pressed you in that direction more than it ought under other circumstances."

"I can certainly not deny it, Hamish, but in any case, Edwin McNee needs be pulled down a peg or two. If this opportunity is missed, I fear it will go badly for Mrs. McNee. It seems my entry into this situation is coincidental, though mayhap fortuitous, at least for her."

"And for yourself?"

"That is for Providence to decide."

"Hmmm…Be wary, lad. You may best McNee in this endeavor, and I suspect you will, but he is a powerful man nonetheless, and may create his own opportunities to repay the favor if a prospect presents itself. I have limited experience with such folk, but know the powerful and mighty have long memories."

I thought about that as we walked and of course, Hamish was right. My interference would certainly create McNee's lifelong enmity; of that, I could be sure. But I had committed myself and would not turn back. Whatever the future held,

I would confront in due course. I thanked Hamish again for the tobacco, the arrangements he had made for the evening, and bade him goodnight.

In the morning, whilst enjoying a pot of tea and my first pipe of the day, I wrote out three telegrams I would send on my way to the Baines residence. One was to Inspector MacLeish asking the current whereabouts of Grimes and Bellows, the second to Seamus McGivern, a fellow inquiry agent in Belfast, and the third to Edwin McNee. The one to McNee was short but I felt sure to prompt the response I wanted. It read: **SUBJECT FOUND. IF YOU ARRIVE KENDAL WEDNESDAY, WILL ARRANGE FOR RECOVERY OF LOST ITEMS THURSDAY. PITT.**

Two days should be ample time for McNee to travel to Kendal. One long day might be sufficient but I suspected McNee wasn't given to long travel days. In any event, I expected a quick response.

I posted the wires on the way to the Baines residence and having rung the bell, stood waiting for a moment at their front door. I couldn't help but think of how pleasant it would be to see Mrs. McNee again. I was quite taken with her, fully aware of it, and prompted myself to be on guard against interfering emotions that could compromise any action we might take.

Jameson opened the door. "Good morning, Mr. Pitt."

"Good morning, Jameson. Mr. Baines is expecting me, I believe."

"Yes sir. He's in his office."

Jameson took my hat and coat after I'd removed pipe and tobacco pouch and I followed him down the hallway. Arthur Baines was sitting at his desk, pipe in hand, reading a single sheet of paper that lay in front of him. He looked up as I came in, smiled, and came around from behind the desk to greet me.

"If you don't mind my asking," I said, "how in the world did you manage to get a desk of that size into this room?"

"Didn't. Had the damn thing made to my specifications right where it sits. It suits me. It's of a good size, has some hidden drawers, and a revolver ledge in the alcove. I chuckle when I think of the puzzle it will be for the next owner of this place. If they don't like the desk, they will have to use it for kindling or tear out a wall."

I smiled. "I should think if it were mine, I would leave it. Certainly, it is the focal point of the room which would look bare without it."

We walked to the fireplace and sat down as I began to fill my pipe.

"Tis a fine looking billiard, Joshua. What is it?"

"GBD. I took it in payment for looking into a small theft."

"Resolved successfully, I presume?"

"And somewhat humorously as well."

Baines had brought the document with him from the desk and now handed it to me. It was both specific and vague, a typical solicitor's piece of work. In essence, it said that in return for certain, unnamed considerations on the part of Eileen McNee, Edwin McNee would not oppose a petition for disjunction, nor would he take any adverse action against her or her natural family. In addition, he would agree to remit to her four hundred pounds, in promptitude, that she may resettle where she chose.

"In promptitude?"

Baines paused lighting his pipe. "As I understand it, that means within thirty days, though it is often sooner. Wealthy as he is, McNee may balk at loosening his purse strings under duress, though threatened with exposure of some of his more shady business dealings, I am sure he will relent. How do you plan to proceed?"

I chuckled. "With lies and duplicity. I wired him this morning asking that he come to Kendal Wednesday; that we should be able to resolve everything Thursday. Since both your daughter and Mrs. McNee are accomplished horsewomen, I think a short excursion to the grounds of Parr Castle at midday Thursday would be in order. Mrs. McNee will carry the blackthorn. Her husband and I will have arrived early and when the ladies dismount to explore the grounds, we shall *confront* them. At least that is what McNee will think. At that point, Mrs. McNee can present him with the divorce agreement. I expect him to quickly realize he has been set up and in all likelihood will attempt to vent his anger on me and not the women. His reaction is impossible to predict, however, and given his past proclivity for attacking a defenseless woman, he may try to do so again. In any event, I shall be prepared for that."

"I should certainly like to see that," said Baines, "but think it unwise to be an active participant."

"I was hoping you would say that. Credible witnesses could be of future value. I thought perhaps you and Hamish could conceal yourselves beforehand and observe the festivities, as it were."

Arthur Baines laughed. "I think you take great pleasure in this."

I smiled in return. "Some, I suppose. It is not often I have the opportunity to see a scoundrel, who in all events is untouchable in any other way, receive his comeuppance." I paused for a moment, thinking, and my silence was noticed by Baines.

"Something has occurred to you?"

"I think it was a Scotsman who once said something like, 'knowledge without fact is mere speculation,' though I can't remember who it might have been. Our knowledge of the McNee case is provisional and one sided. We have Mrs. McNee's accusations and evidence of bruises which we assume were caused as the result of one or more beatings by her husband, but we have no proof. Like a frog leaping from one lily pad to another, I jumped from an immediate dislike of McNee, to the handsome and winning ways of his wife, to belief in her story."

Baines looked astonished. "Do you mean to say you disbelieve her?"

"No, not at all. What I am saying is that I have no proof, or at least, corroboration. I hope to receive information today or tomorrow, latest, that will confirm her charges. In the meantime, we shall move forward. I would like to talk with her and your daughter."

Baines left the room and in the interim, I took time to light my pipe and reflect upon the situation whilst staring into the embers of the coal fire that had burned down to a soft glow. I did not for a moment disbelieve Eileen McNee's story but as I had remarked to Baines, I had no proof. I had circumstantial evidence and hearsay, but no concrete facts. At that moment, Baines returned with his daughter and Eileen, and I have to admit, upon seeing her again, fact was relegated to the back recesses of my mind. She was in a white ankle length dress decorated with small, pale blue flowers, and a scoop neck that gave hint to her womanhood. The heat I felt did not come from the wasted fire in the fireplace. She came forward, smiling, her hand outstretched to bid me good day. I took her hand, holding it longer that propriety might suggest, but was loathe to let go and I'm sure she sensed it. After a few seconds, I relinquished her hand and bade both ladies sit by the fireplace. I stood at the mantle taking occasional puffs on my pipe whilst explaining their role in what I had planned for Thursday. Though I had only been to Parr castle once, I remembered a courtyard just inside the ruined walls on the south side and told them I felt the meeting with McNee would be to our advantage if it took place in those confined quarters. I impressed upon Mrs. McNee that above all, she should have the blackthorn and the prepared document with her but both should be out of sight when they arrived. The document should be in her purse and the blackthorn placed in a sleeve attached to the saddle. It was not until they dismounted that I would make an appearance with her husband. They both had a few questions but they were of small detail and little consequence. Tea was served whilst we talked and eventually the conversation turned away from Thursday's task to objects more of a mundane nature. Both ladies were curious as to how and why I had become an inquiry agent and I provided a few highlights including my friendship with Sherlock Holmes and the

Honorable John Watson, MD and author. Eventually, and I must admit, reluctantly, I took my leave and returned to the Inn.

There, I was met by Hamish who was standing by the main desk, chatting with the landlord. I had intended to call upon him later in the day and ask him to accompany Arthur Baines to Parr Castle Thursday, but his unexpected appearance saved me a trip and I told him so, explaining that I had been to the Baines residence.

He smiled, put a match to his pipe and around the stem, asked, "Have you been courtin' this morning already, lad?"

Before I could make a caustic reply, he went on to say, "Just joshing you lad, just joshing, but I saw a sparkle in your eye when you met the Lady McNee last evening. Aye, tis a fine looking woman there."

I realized, of course, that any reply would simply give him another opening so I chose to ignore his remark and instead, begged some tobacco. As I filled my pipe, I turned to the landlord. "I'm expecting some telegrams. I think we'll step into the pub for a drink and afterwards will be in my room. Would you bring them to me when they arrive? There should be three I all."

"There was one delivered not more than ten minutes ago, Mr. Pitt." He pulled a folded sheet of paper from my room box and handed it to me. I took it and we walked into the adjoining hotel bar. We seated ourselves at a table, both ordered a pint, and then unfolded the wire. It was from McNee and short: **WILL ARRIVE WEDNESDAY AFTERNOON. ARRANGE ACCOMODATIONS. EDWIN MCNEE.** I handed it to Hamish.

"No a well mannered bastard, is he? No even a thank you. Were I you, lad, I would put him up in some other hotel."

"Oh, I think it makes little difference. He is disagreeable in any case. Will you join Mr. Baines on Thursday?"

"Delighted. This is the most excitement I have had in a year and I would nae miss it for the world."

We both lit our pipes and over the remainder of our pints, I filled him in on what to expect and where I thought he and Baines could secret themselves, yet be close enough to see and hear all that went on. We were about to order sandwiches and another pint when the landlord came from the Inn with responses to my two other telegrams. I opened the first, which was from Inspector MacLeish: **GRIMES AT HIS POST FOR BREAKFAST THIS MORNING AT THE SAVOY. BELLOWS IN IRELAND BUT WHEREABOUTS UNKNOWN. IS THERE SOMETHING I SHOULD KNOW? MACLEISH.** I handed it to Hamish with the remark that I would have reply later and then opened the second. It was from Seamus McGivern in Belfast. I had asked if he could quietly confirm rumors of McNee's brutish behavior toward his wife. His reply was what I had hoped: **COMMON KNOWLEDGE AMONG MCNEE DOMESTIC STAFF. INQUIRY SUGGESTS MRS HAS GONE MISSING. FOLLOWUP? MCGIVERN.** I passed it to Hamish who read it, then glanced up at me. "Weel, lad, it confirms what you have heard. Did you have any doubts?"

"I had no proof. And though this can hardly be called proof, at least it salves my conscience. I suspect McNee's reaction when confronted by his wife will be proof enough."

We finished lunch and I declined Hamish's offer of mid afternoon fishing in favor of repairing to my room to do some much needed thinking and perhaps a nap. On my way, I stopped at the hotel desk, made arrangements for a room for McNee, and sent wires to MacLeish and McGivern saying that nothing more was required at this time and thanked them both. Once in my room, I poured myself a whiskey, set my tobacco pouch on the table near the bed, cleaned the pipe I had been smoking all morning and exchanged it for another from a small leather case that held several. Thus prepared, I propped two pillows against the headboard and lay back, thinking of another man's wife. I woke two hours later, as much confused as when I drifted off. I filled and lit my pipe and not having touched the whiskey, poured it back in the bottle. A pot of strong tea is what I was wanting, so I walked downstairs to the kitchen to ask the cook if she had any Assam, and if so, would she be kind enough to fix a pot for me. She had and she did, and I returned to my room with a scone in addition to the tea.

I was very strongly attracted to Eileen McNee and believed she was attracted to me as well, but had no way to measure the depth of her feeling at this point. I was also aware that any overt display of feeling on our part would be inappropriate, not to say improper. Her treatment at the hands of her husband aside, she was a married woman and that in itself posed serious concern for her reputation. After much consideration, a bowl of tobacco and the entire pot of tea, I decided that I must do whatever was necessary to keep everything above board and businesslike, though friendly. If the opportunity arose, however, I would make my feelings known and at least hint at a deeper relationship in the future. A frustrating decision, to be sure, but the only proper one.

The next two days were quiet ones for the most part and I began to feel as if I truly were on holiday. I spent the morning of the first day wandering around Kendal, stopping for a while at Samuel Gawith Tobaccos to chat and purchase two pounds of tobacco. The late afternoon was spent fishing with Hamish, followed by supper at his cottage of two of the trout we caught in the cold rushing waters of the River Kent.

On the morning of the second day, I went first to Parr Castle to familiarize myself with the grounds and the area where our little drama would play out. The courtyard was much as I remembered but more littered with stones and slightly larger than memory had defined for me. There were several hiding places within sight and earshot for Hamish and Baines and a partially standing wall to accommodate myself and McNee whilst we waited for the ladies to arrive on horseback. The castle itself was remote but not far, and rarely visited by townfolk, so I felt we would not be disturbed. I felt comfortable with the precautions taken and hoped all would be accomplished without a hitch. I expected anger from McNee but he was certainly an intelligent man and I expected him to quickly realize his cause was lost and to accede to his wife's terms, consequential as they may be in his social world. Having no solid evidence of his complicity in any stock market schemes with Grimes and Bellows, I could only imply that I had if it came to that. Public charges of spousal brutality were a different matter, however, and something I felt he would want to avoid at any cost. His own self-image and vanity might lend a hand.

Early afternoon was spent at the Baines Manor where I succeeded in keeping my feelings for Eileen in check though some meaningful looks passed between us, or at least I took them to be. I left the residence soon after three o'clock and walked back to the Inn. As it happened, I was talking with the landlord and debating a pint in the bar when a carriage drew up outside and Edwin McNee alighted. He was in a blustery mood, dusty from travel and imperious, which was his nature in any case.

"Did you arrange a room, Pitt?"

"I did. Two doors from my own."

There being few guests, I could have arranged for him to be in the room next to mine but that was asking too much of me in my present frame of mind. The coachman brought in two bags, tipped his hat to the landlord and returned to his carriage without waiting for a tip. He had read McNee correctly and realized early on that a tip would not be forthcoming. McNee signed the register and we proceeded to his room which was a pleasant one, I thought, and slightly larger than my own. McNee walked around, felt the bed and muttered a remark about cramped quarters before turning to me.

"I should like to see my wife this evening. No…I demand to see her this evening!"

"I think that unwise, Mr. McNee, and in all events, probably impossible. My sources tell me she is away with the Baines this evening having dinner at a neighbor's farm." A blatant lie of course, but a necessary one. I was not about to have our plans for the morrow confounded by his arrogance.

"I don't give a damn what you think, Pitt. You are in my employ and I expect you to render your services to me as directed. Now, where is this farm?"

Inadvertently, I had prepared for this eventuality. I had been operating on my own funds, intending to deposit McNee's cheque when I returned to London. I took the envelope containing the cheque from my coat pocket and tossed it on the table.

"Your cheque, McNee." I had dropped the *Mister*. "Find your own wife and conduct your own affairs." I caught the stunned expression on his face as I turned toward the door and before I could open it, he coughed and muttered something unintelligible that sounded like a vulgar curse.

"Wait, Pitt...wait."

I stopped with my hand on the door handle but didn't respond. His anger was apparent in the redness of his face but I had to admire his control. He sat down on the edge of the bed and turned slightly toward me.

"As much as it grates on me, I'm forced to accede to your course of action. I had hoped to see my wife and recover my blackthorn this evening, then return to Ireland with both on the morrow. Your telegram interrupted some delicate business negotiations and I am anxious to return and conclude them but it seems I have no choice...What is your plan for the morning?"

I stepped back away from the door but made no move to recover the cheque. "My informant tells me your wife and Miss Baines will be riding to Parr Castle tomorrow and should be there about noon. I am also reliably informed that Mrs. McNee is never seen away from the Parr residence without your blackthorn in her possession and I fully expect her to have it with her when riding in the morning. We shall leave the Inn early enough that we can be on the castle grounds when they arrive and you may confront her then."

"I seems straight forward, that is if your information is good."

"It is as good as we will get." I again turned toward the door. "I shall be otherwise occupied this evening, but will see you tomorrow morning at about ten o'clock." I opened the door and stepped into the hallway before he could respond.

Upon entering my room, I poured two fingers of whiskey from a bottle Arthur Baines had been kind enough to give me, and then filled an lit a pipe. I sat for a few moments, taking short puffs on my pipe whilst staring vacantly through the small mullioned window that looked out onto the hotel grounds. Had McNee called my bluff and gone charging over to the Baines residence, I'm not sure what would have ensued, but surely there would have been violence. Confrontation would have taken place, not only with Eileen had McNee got that far, but most certainly with Arthur Baines. I would have been blamed and rightly so.

I finished my whiskey and set my pipe on the small table next to my bed whilst donning my Ulster and hat. Pocketing my tobacco pouch with a spare pipe, and with another pipe in my mouth leaving puffs of smoke behind me resembling a locomotive, I set out for Hamish's cottage. When I arrived, a light tap with the knocker brought him to the door, glass in hand.

"I were just havin' a wee drop. Would you care to join me?"

"I would. There is a dampness in the air this evening. I hope it doesn't rain in the morning—might set McNee to wondering why the ladies would venture out."

"Aye…weel, from what little I know of him, he is nae a man with much imagination. He will be tinkin' of his stick and draggin' his wife back to home and hearth."

I smiled. "He wanted to attend to that business this evening. I threatened to quit him and he reconsidered."

"And a good ting, too. A rough-and-tumble at the manor is not something Baines would want, though tis something he might relish. He should be here soon."

I wanted to be sure of our timing if Hamish and Baines were to be present, as well as a place where they could observe but remain out of sight. "Do you have pencil and paper, Hamish? I want to sketch out the part of the castle grounds where the meeting should take place and where you should be to see and hear."

He had both and I proceeded to draw a reasonable facsimile of the courtyard area. I had just finished when there was a knock at the door. It was Arthur Baines in ulster, hat, and scarf muffled round.

Hamish stood back and then closed the door. "Dressed a wee bit warmly for this time of year, are you not?"

"I'm afraid I've caught a chill but nothing serious. Nothing that a bit of whiskey mightn't make better."

Hamish provided the whiskey and afterwards, using the stem of my pipe, I pointed out where I thought they could seclude themselves, yet remain within earshot and sight of the meeting. There were the remains of two sets of false walls at one end of the courtyard and though the distance was perhaps seventy feet, I thought it would be close enough.

"Will we be close enough to overhear?" asked Baines.

"I think so," said I. "McNee is not given to using a soft voice for anything, though I'm not sure you will be able to hear Mrs. McNee. When you return home, you might ask her to speak up a bit when she confronts her husband. Given the situation, it might be the normal thing to do and I doubt he would consider it suspicious."

Hamish poured another tot of whiskey for us, then we all three lit our pipes and sat round the table discussing the adventure of the morrow as well as weather and the effect on fishing. Baines and myself took our leave after an hour and I walked part way with him toward his home.

"You should have taken a trap," said I, "having a chill and all."

"I thought of it but then decided not, hoping the walk and the air would do me some good. I have been in the house all day." He paused for a moment, then went on. "I couldn't help but notice there is some affection between you and Eileen. There was an immediate rapport and a hint of future promise. I would urge caution, at least for now. Her emotions are quite frayed and I am afraid she looks upon you as her knight errant. A normal response, no doubt, but nonetheless…"

"You do not know me well, Mr. Baines, so it might surprise you that I quite agree with you. I should like very much to know her on a more intimate level, but this is neither the time nor the place. I would ask a favor of you, however. I assume she will remain as your guest for a while after this affair is closed. If so, I should like to write to her in your care after I return to London. Would that meet with your approval?"

"Most certainly. And please, call me Arthur. Mr. Baines is much too formal for a couple of co-conspirators in an adventure."

We both laughed and then parted ways. As I entered the Inn, I noticed McNee in the bar and having no wish to see or talk with him, hurried up the stairs to my room. I would see him soon enough in the morning.

I was awake early, completed my toilet, and broke my fast with tea and buttered scones. I had considered a heartier meal of eggs and a rasher but thought it too heavy for what the morning had in store. After finishing my second cup of tea, I donned coat and hat, lit my pipe and left the inn for a short walk along the river. The day held promise. Though cool, the skies were clear and pale blue with no clouds in sight to the west. Trout were nosing the top waters of deeper pools along the bank, though for what insects, I couldn't tell. The thought occurred to me then, that if I returned to London the following day, I would not have a chance to find out. Well, perhaps an extra day…And I had to admit that an extra day would provide an opportunity to perhaps talk with Eileen without the cloud of her husband hanging over her head.

I returned to the inn, half expecting to see McNee in the dining room but there was no sign of him. Perhaps he was already out and about or more likely, still sleeping off last evening's whiskey. I begged a pot of tea from the cook and returned to my room wanting to relax but was nervous with anticipation of the coming events. I read for a while but as it neared ten o'clock, with no word from McNee, I decided to check on him.

I could hear loud snoring as I stood outside the door to his room. I will not admit to an evil grin on my face as I banged loudly on the door but mentally, it was certainly there. There was a snort, a curse, and then an outraged, "Who is there?"

"Pitt," I said loudly through the door, "and if you expect to see your wife today, you had better jump to it. It is almost ten."

More cursing and then I could hear him come toward the door. Through it, he asked in a voice still thick with sleep and last night's drink, "Would you be kind enough to ask them to send up a pot of coffee?"

"I will. I am going to make arrangements for a trap and we will leave at eleven." I went downstairs, asked that a pot of coffee be sent to McNee's room and secured transportation for us for eleven o'clock. Afterwards, I stepped outside, lit my pipe and smiled in recollection. "Aye, tis going to be a bonnie day," as Hamish would say.

At a few minutes before eleven, McNee came downstairs into the lobby, still looking grey and out of sorts, but presentable. We exchanged good mornings and climbed aboard the trap for the trip to Parr Castle, which was no more than fifteen minutes, but I was right in assuming McNee would be in no fit shape for the walk.

I was lighting my pipe when he turned to me. "Are you sure they will be there?"

"I cannot be certain, of course, but the information I have received so far has been correct. I was told if the day was a pleasant one, your wife would accompany Mr. Baines daughter on a ride to the castle. Since it is a nice day, I assume they will be there."

He said no more for the remainder of the trip. We arrived on the far side of the castle grounds from where we would be going and I asked the driver to wait, telling him it would be an hour or more, but he would be amply compensated. I preferred the driver to be out of sight and earshot. We walked for slightly more than five minutes before I took McNee's arm and held him at the corner of the outside wall to the courtyard. I looked round but could not see Hamish and Arthur Baines, though if they were hidden where we had planned, I would not.

"We will wait here." I had no more than spoken when off at a distance of perhaps a quarter mile, we could see two riders moving toward the castle. Still holding McNee's arm, I continued, "I have been led to understand this courtyard is a favorite place of Miss Baines and expect this is where they will come. Let them dismount and settle before you show yourself. I suspect it may be a more difficult task to convince your wife to return to Ireland with you than to recover your blackthorn, but that is none of my affair for the present."

"My stick, yes, and I'll have that bitch too!"

The vehemence with which he said it should not have surprised me but it did. I feared then, that I may have made a mistake and if any harm should befall Eileen McNee, it would be my fault. I would not let that happen.

The ladies entered the courtyard, dismounted, and were leading their horses to a post to tie them off when McNee rushed the forty feet or so to his wife. The blackthorn was in a scabbard attached to the saddle and McNee pulled it loose as he forcefully shoved his wife to the ground and raised the stick high above his head. I was just close enough behind and tall enough to snap the stick from his hand in a leap that put me next to Eileen. He turned to me in a rage, his face red and twisted in anger.

"You are taking liberties, you bastard! You are in my employ…"

"I returned your cheque to you yesterday. I am my own man!"

It was too much for him. He rushed me with both fists raised, his indignant wroth now directed at me and not his wife. I stepped to one side and as he came past, laid the heavy cudgel hard across his back and he went down. Before he could rise, I twice laid the lighter end of the blackthorn across his shoulders and he stayed put. I stepped back and reached out my hand to help Eileen to her feet.

"Are you alright, Miss?"

"Yes, I think so." Turning toward McNee, in a mocking voice, she said, "This is the great Lord of McNee Manor, face on the cobbles and in the dirt after attacking a woman. It is where you belong!"

McNee rolled over on his back then moved to a sitting position, unsure if I would strike again if he made move to rise. "I would have my blackthorn."

"You will have your precious stick," said Eileen, "but in return for something more precious to me—my freedom." She handed him the divorce document that had been prepared by Baines' solicitor.

He took it, read through it, and then threw it on the ground. "You will have your freedom—never!"

He made to rise and raising the blackthorn, I ordered him to stay put. "You would be wise, I think, to reconsider. I am fully aware of your involvement in stock manipulations with Grimes and Bellows and have no doubt the pressing business you wish to return to in Ireland is with Bellows. I am not above passing on those details to Scotland Yard." I picked up the document and held it out to him.

"You blackmailing bastard! I have friends in high places and you'll pay for this, Pitt."

"I have been called worse and by better men, McNee. You may have friends in high places, sir, but so do I, and I suspect if Her Majesty learns you're a wife beater, you've seen the last of your horses in the Royal Stables. I also have friends in low places who might deem it more fitting to take justice into their own hands…"

"Is that a threat, Pitt?"

"That it is, McNee, that it is, and not an idle one. I suggest you sign."

He took the document, reread it and then fished a fountain pen from inside his coat and scribbled his signature at the bottom. "I suppose you will be a signed witness to this?"

"Only if need be but I think Miss Baines as a witness will be sufficient."

"How do I know you will not give information regarding my business dealings to Scotland Yard?"

"You have my word, which I dare say is a damned sight better than yours. As long as you keep to this agreement…" What I did not say, of course, was that all that I had was circumstantial and conjecture but McNee did not have to know that.

He handed the paper to me and I in turn, handed it to Eileen. As I did, he made move to rise and I threw the cudgel at him. He picked it up, rose from the cobbles and half raised the blackthorn toward me. I took a step forward. "Try it, and I'll take that stick from you, break it in half, and cram it up your arse!" I think we both believed I would do it…

Eileen and Mary set out for the Baines residence while I stood by keeping an eye on McNee. After they had gone some distance, I drew my pipe from my pocket, tamped and lit it, and turned to him. "You can take the trap back alone. I'll walk." He did not say anything immediately, but looked at me for a moment before placing the blackthorn under his left arm.

"You are a hard man, Pitt, I'll give you credit for that. And smarter than I was led to believe." With that, he turned and walked away.

I watched him go, waited a few moments and then walked to the crest of a knoll on the west side of the castle wall where I observed him get into the trap and head back to Kendal. So lost in thought was I that I didn't hear Hamish and Arthur Baines approach until Hamish said, "Twas quite a ta-do, laddie. Arthur was all for lending a hand but I held him back." I turned and Hamish had a wide grin on his face. "I tink he just wanted a crack at McNee."

I was not smiling. "I don't trust that sod."

"Nor do I," said Baines, "but I think he'll agree to the terms in the agreement he signed. He has too much to lose if not. My mistrust is in the matter of what moves he may eventually make against you, and I fully expect him to do that."

"As do I, but not soon. He is one who will bide his time."

We returned to the Baines manor in his coach and there met Eileen and Mary who had arrived just a few minutes ahead of us. Mary went off with her father and Hamish, leaving Eileen and myself a few moments alone to talk.

"I don't know how to thank you, Joshua. Whatever would have happened to me if you had not come into my life, I do not know. Will you be returning to London soon?"

I reached out and touched her cheek with my fingertips. "On the morrow, perhaps, but the next day for certain. I have business to attend to."

She took hold of my hand and kissed my palm. Swept up with emotion, I slipped my arm around her tiny waist, pulled her close and we kissed, both giving into passion. Then she stepped back, still holding my hands, and smiling. "There was a promise in that kiss, Joshua."

"There was, and if you will allow me, I will keep it one day. For now, however, it is best that we keep some distance between us, like it or not. Any public sign of affection between us might compromise your petition and Edwin McNee would like nothing more. Far better we be apart for a time than to place you back in his reach."

So we left it like that. I returned to London the following day but we write each other often and I expect to be in Kendal as a guest of Arthur Baines for some early spring fishing…among other things.

And as it turned out, that snowy evening in London, my telling of the tale so took Dr. Watson that I won the last two games of chess.

END

THE CASE OF THE GLASGOW HORROR

Joshua Pitt glanced over the top of his newspaper, caught the eye of the stall-keeper, and nodded his head. In a moment, a fresh, steaming cup of hot coffee was sitting in front of him. It was mid evening, late Spring, and had been an unusually warm and beautiful day in London with flowers blooming in a profusion of color no matter where he looked, and he seemed to have looked everywhere. It had been a lazy day, one with no developments in the two active cases he had and no new cases to call his attention to, so by mid afternoon he decided a walk was in order. He window-shopped his way to the Strand, lost track of time, and before he knew it, evening was upon him. Spying a newspaper stand next to a coffee stall, he picked up a *Times* evening edition and settled in at a table for a cup of coffee and bowl of tobacco.

World or national events headlined on the front page held no interest for him and he turned to the agony columns. Many of these snippets were written in cipher and he enjoyed trying to puzzle them out, so he whiled away the best part of an hour, three cups of coffee, and a full pipe while scribbling solutions and translations on a piece of paper. Comedy and tragedy often alternated and some of the more straight-forward ones could produce a frown or a smile: "*Lady with auburn hair in food court at M&S Tuesday morning. Gentleman desires introductions. Reply here.*" or "*With child. Father has obtained warrant. Leave city. MS.*" The one that eventually caught his eye, however, appeared in plain English and bespoke of interesting possibilities. It read simply, "*Celia and Fiona pursued. Glas-*

gow Horror. Help. Reply this department." The appeal piqued his interest, not only because of his Scottish roots but because he'd heard of the Glasgow Horror many years before from his mother.

He'd been a young lad then, still living in Glasgow, and his mother had commented once that she would not leave the flat after dark. When Joshua asked why, she replied, "Tis the Glasgow Horror, a bad man wot preys on women come nighttime." But that had been years ago, perhaps fifteen, just after his father died and they left for London on the promise his mother would have a job as a seamstress. But the job turned out to be slaving in a sweatshop making uniforms for nurses, waitresses, maids and other housekeeping staff. Joshua continued his schooling and she worked, but when he was little more than sixteen, she died and he took to the streets, sometimes running with a ragamuffin gang of boys known as the Baker Street Irregulars, a name given them by Mr. Sherlock Holmes, who occasionally paid a few shillings for odd jobs.

After moving to London, he had read some vague newspaper reports of the Horror that gave few details other than he attacked mostly prostitutes living in and working the streets near the docks. Three of his victims, however, had been young housewives in middleclass neighborhoods. He used a knife, sometimes slashing and sometimes simply cutting their throats and quickly leaving his victim to bleed to death. He was never caught, but after four years and eleven murdered women, the attacks stopped in 1883. In some respects, the attacks of the Glasgow Horror were mirrored some five years later by Jack the Ripper in Whitechapel, though Pitt could hardly believe there was any connection. And now this personal in the times. He wondered if Inspector MacLeish had seen it.

He finished his coffee, cleaned his pipe, and then slipped it into his pocket before he stood, stretched, and crossed the street to the Charing Cross Hotel. Entering, he walked to the alcove that housed several tables, writing paper, and envelopes. Using one of the scratchy hotel pens, he wrote, "*Regarding your personal in the Times, this date, am offering assistance. Joshua Pitt, Inquiry agent. 22C Baker Street, Regent's Park.*" He sealed the envelope, addressed it appropriately, and took it to the desk clerk to be mailed. Outside once again, he paused long enough to fill and light his pipe before walking back to his rooms in Baker Street. Perhaps Celia and Fiona would answer, or perhaps not. If they did, however, the case of the Glasgow Horror had the mark of an interesting adventure.

Mrs. Keating, his landlady, was sitting at the dining room table drinking a cup of tea when he came through the door.

"Did you have a nice walk, then, Mr. Pitt?"

"Yes, very nice. I'm afraid the three cups of coffee I indulged myself in may require a wee dram of whiskey and a pipe to counteract the effects, though. There will be no need of my evening pot of tea so I'll bid you good night, Mrs Keating.

"And a good night to you, sir; sleep well."

He did not. He suspected it was the coffee but something had contributed to a restless period of nightmares. Nameless grotesque faces, women running and screaming from some unseen terror, blood on the streets and in the gutters—the gutters awash with blood. The last time he could remember having such dreams was when on his first voyage, his ship put in to Liverpool and he got roaring drunk with a bunch of the lads for the first time. He had been far more judicious with his use of alcohol since. Then he remembered the notice in the newspaper and assumed it was a combination of coffee and suggestion brought on by the call for help from two women.

There was a knock at his sitting room door and from his bedroom, he heard it open. Mrs. Keating with his tea and buttered scones, he was sure.

"Good morning, Mr. Pitt."

"Good morning, Mrs. Keating."

"Seven o'clock and sunshine. Not a cloud in the sky."

"Thank you," was about all he could muster. He felt groggy, as if he had not slept in a week. He paid his required morning visit to the WC, washed his face and hands and feeling some better sat at his desk and poured a cup of Assam tea. The heady aroma and taste of the tea helped even more, as did the scone, so that upon finishing his first cup he rose and went to the bookcase to select a pipe and tobacco. He debated between a large bent Peterson and a Charatan billiard and finally decided on the Charatan. He filled the pipe with Arcadia blend, returned to his desk, and unfolded his copy of *The Times*. The headlines were as usual but at the bottom of the front page a leader caught his eye; **MURDER IN THE STRAND**. It was short, with not much information, but read:

> *The body of a young woman later identified as Celia MacLaurin, of Glasgow Scotland, was discovered at approximately ten o'clock last night by a constable on his beat on Savoy Street near the Embankment. She had been stabbed repeatedly and had expired by the time the constable arrived on the scene. Inspectors MacLeish and Bell of Scotland Yard have been placed in charge of the investigation.*

He read it through once before tamping, relighting his pipe and reading it again. It had to be the Celia from the agony column of yesterday. It had to be! Newspaper in hand and still in his robe, he went downstairs in search of Mrs.

Keating. She was in the kitchen and he asked her to send her boy to fetch a cab and bring it round immediately. "Tell him Fin, if his cab is available!"

He rushed back upstairs, changed into street clothes, filled a tobacco pouch from a glass jar, and put pouch and two pipes in his jacket pocket before walking back downstairs with yesterday's newspaper under his arm. He arrived at the front door as a hansom circled round in the street and pulled to the kerb. It was Fin.

"Mornin' gov'nor. Where we be off to, then?"

"Scotland Yard, Fin, and I'll want you to wait."

"Right ya are. Settle yourself an' ole Fin'll 'ave ya there in a jiff."

The trip was not a long one, but bumpy over the cobbles, and he managed to somehow light a pipe and tuck himself back into the pedestrian corner of the cab. At an angle, he watched slices of London move by the window; people from all walks of life on journeys to nowhere or somewhere. He always marveled at the inhabitants of London. From the richest to the poorest, from the banker to the prostitute, under the skin they were all cut from the same cloth: resolute and made of stern stuff. Shopkeepers were just opening their doors, newspapers were being hawked on street corners, finely dressed gentlemen moved around still sleeping drunks propped against building walls. Joshua couldn't help himself; he loved this city.

Fin pulled to the kerb in front of the Yard and as Pitt stepped out of the cab, said with a wave, "I'll be ta stand at yon corner."

"Fine, Fin. Thank you."

He entered the building and walked down the hallway to the shared office of MacLeish and Bell. They were both in, Bell just slipping on his coat as Pitt entered and MacLeish pouring himself a cup of tea from an old brown pot.

"Would ya be havin' a cuppa, laddie?"

"Just finished one, but thank you anyway."

"So...What'd be bringing Mr. Pitt ta the Yard so early in the morning, then?"

"The Glasgow Horror."

MacLeish stopped pouring and Bell paused in the doorway, then turned and walked back into the room.

Pitt took a pipe from his pocket but made no attempt to light it. "From the look on both your faces, I would guess it is a name heard recently...last night, perhaps? Perhaps from a woman named Fiona?"

MacLeish set the pot down. "Better 'ave a seat, lad, an' tell us just 'ow you 'appen to know about this."

Pitt took a seat beside the desk and laid his copy of last evening's newspaper in front of MacLeish. He'd circled the personal from Fiona and Celia. While MacLeish read it, Bell looking over his shoulder, he lit his pipe. When MacLeish looked up at him, Pitt said, "I answered the advertisement last evening offering my services."

He then went on to tell them how he'd seen the personal, remembered the Glasgow Horror from his childhood and that it piqued his interest, though he couldn't imagine the women being pursued by the same person who'd slaughtered the women in Glasgow years ago.

"Nor do we, Mr. Pitt," said Bell. "But the young woman, Fiona, sister to the woman who was killed last evening, is insistent. Not only insistent, but terrified. She claims their mother was murdered by the Horror in Glasgow when they were just young girls and now he is back after all these years."

"Do you believe her?"

"Weel, laddie…" MacLeish picked up an old bent pipe from his desk and filled it from his pouch. "Tis nowt tha we nae believe 'er, ya understand, but 'im comin back after all these years strains the mind as it were."

"That was my thought," said Pitt, "but from the newspaper account in this morning's paper, it would appear she may be right. The report in the newspaper said she was murdered about ten o'clock. Is that right?

"Aye, she were discovered aboot ten, but some of the blood had dried on her dress an' we be tinkin' it were closer to nine o'clock she were attacked."

Could I possibly talk with the sister, Fiona?"

He could see reluctance in Bell's face, but MacLeish said, "We 'ave 'id ta lass away, like…as a precaution ya understand, but seein' as ya been of assistance tae us on several occasions in the past, mayhap you can help in this instance."

MacLeish's tacit approval quelled any reticence on Bell's part and they were soon on the way in Fin's hansom to a small boarding house on Compton Street in Soho. Little was said on the trip but when they turned onto Charing Cross Road, MacLeish leaned out the window to ask Fin to stop in the middle of the next block.

Pitt turned to MacLeish. "Is there a problem?"

"Aye, laddie, a big one. I'm out of tobacco and there's a wee shop tha' I frequent in the next block." They all laughed and if there was any tension among the group, it was broken by MacLeish's need for tobacco. After a short stop of a few minutes whilst Mac's tobacco pouch was replenished with a couple ounces of shag, they were on their way again and a few minutes later the hansom pulled to the kerb in front of a moderate red brick home—one of several identical houses that formed a row at the end of a tree lined street. If it was a boarding house in the normal sense, there was no outward indication by any sign in front and Pitt suspected it might be one of several around the city used by the police force to house informants or witnesses they wanted to keep out of sight for a while. This was more or less confirmed when a man Pitt had seen on occasion at the Yard answered the door to Bell's knock. He was introduced to Pitt simply as Tom, and they were then led to a room on the ground floor where they paused while MacLeish knocked softly at the door and announced, "Miss MacLaurin, tis Inspector MacLeish."

The door was opened by a young woman in her twenties wearing a dark blue dress with white lace piping at the sleeve ends and collar. She was quite attractive, or so Pitt thought. Tall and slender, with straw-blonde hair pulled and braided into a single plait that reached almost to mid back, and features that bespoke of Scandinavian somewhere in her ancestry. Her dark brown eyes, red now from what Pitt took to be recent crying, took them in as she opened the door wide to admit them. Though a Londoner for many years, Pitt was introduced to her as a fellow Scot who assisted the police on occasion and had offered his services in this instance.

"In fact," said Pitt, "I responded to your personal in yesterday's Times but I'm sure circumstances have not permitted you to know that as yet."

She said nothing, but walked to a small round table in the corner of the room and sat down. MacLeish turned to Tom and asked if they could have a pot of tea before taking a seat at the same table and motioning Pitt to do the same. Bell remained standing near the window where he moved the curtain slightly to look outside.

"Now, Miss," MacLeish said gently, "if you could just give Mr. Pitt some background as tae what led up to the tragic event of last evening…"

Taking a handkerchief from her sleeve, she held it up to her eyes for a few seconds, then dropping her hands to her lap, she turned slightly to face Pitt, looking at him—not seeing him, composing her thoughts.

"My sister and I are twins…" She paused again and Pitt was sure she didn't know whether to refer to her sister in the past tense, or perhaps bring herself to do so.

Gently, he said, "Go on Miss…"

"My sister and I are twins. We were born and raised in Glasgow in an upper middle class neighborhood, for our father was a successful manager of several dockside warehouses. We were just young girls when our mother was attacked and killed by the Glasgow Horror. That was early in 1883. It was late evening and she was outside the warehouse waiting on father when she was dragged into an alleyway and…and…" She paused again, taking a ragged breath.

Tom came in at that moment carrying a pot of tea, cups, milk and sugar on a tray. He sat a cup in front of Miss MacLaurin and poured. She added a bit of milk, took a sip and then continued.

"Father was never the same. He took heavy to drink, though not around my sister and I, but we could tell…Two years later, he was killed in a loading accident at one of the warehouses. Whether it was the drink or not, or just carelessness, we never knew. But all life had gone out of him after mother died and I don't think he wanted to live, or perhaps didn't care…" She paused again for another sip of tea.

Pitt took his pipe from his pocket. "Would you mind…?"

"No, no, I love the smell of pipe smoke. Father smoked a pipe…"

Pitt filled his pipe, lit it, and leaned back in his chair. "What happened to you after your father died? You were to young, I should think, to be on your own."

"We were given to the care of aunt Maude, a maiden aunt. We called her that anyway. She was my father's younger sister but we were hardly ever in touch before he died. There had been some family quarrel and they didn't get along well, though I think it was more because of her husband than because of her. She was married to a man named Henry Wallace, but a few months after mother was killed, her husband left one morning and never returned. Maude once said he always fancied Australia and she thought he just decided to go one day, though he could have just as well been drunk and fallen off the dock to be washed out to sea. But this has little to do, I think, with current events.

"A fortnight ago, an envelope addressed to my sister and myself as, *The MacLaurin Sisters*, was delivered in the morning post. The few words printed inside terrified us. It read: **I BUTCHERED YOUR MOTHER—NOW IT BE YOUR TURN.** We showed it to aunt Maude; however, she made light of it, saying it was ill humor sent by someone who was certainly daft and she burnt it. But when the second one arrived several days later, she took it more seriously and suggested we should perhaps leave Glasgow for ten days or so and visit London."

MacLeish set his cup on the table and reached for his pipe. "What did the second letter say?"

"It only had one word printed: **SOON**".

"Did ye set about contactin' the police?"

"Aunt Maude went to the police with the second note but of course, we did not have the first one, only our word for what it said. The police dismissed it as the work of a sick person, just as Maude had with the first, but my sister was more upset than I, so when our aunt again suggested a holiday, we traveled to London. That was just five days ago but Celia was still terribly distraught—at wits end you might say—and it was her that put the personal in the paper."

"So, Miss, why was it then, your sister went out alone so late at night?"

"We had a hotplate and kettle in the room but were out of tea. She was going to a confectioner's shop just a block away. It is a decent neighborhood, Inspector. No one would expect…"

Pitt wanted to know how it was that two young women, surely in their early twenties, were still unmarried and living with an aunt but thought such a question might be too personal for the moment. Thinking it more prudent, he posed another. "How is it you could both take a holiday from where you work on such short notice?"

"Oh, neither of us hold a regular position in a factory or office though Celia writes…has written an occasional human interest column for the Sunday Herald. Father's financial holdings were substantial. After his death, the sale of our home added to them, so we were well cared for, though as we grew older we felt aunt Maude to be tight fisted at times. Provision had been made that my sister and I should receive our inheritance when we reached age twenty-two, which is just a month away."

Pitt tamped his pipe, relit it, and over the stem, asked, "And what if either or both of you should marry before your twenty second birthday?"

"The age was fixed at twenty-two, regardless of circumstance."

The next question was an obvious one and since he had no official standing in the case, he felt free to ask it. "Tell me, Miss MacLaurin, if you and your sister were both deceased, would your inheritance fall to your aunt Maude, or to some other member of the family?"

Celia and I both have wills leaving to each other, or in the case of both of us passing away, that our estate should go to several named charities."

Pitt was about to ask another question but was interrupted by a constable who entered carrying a small slip of paper that he handed to MacLeish. Angus glanced at it, then stood. "Shouldnae be takin' more of your time for now, Miss, but may return later. If there be any further developments, we will keep ya informed."

Outside on the steps while MacLeish paused to light his pipe, Pitt did the same and then asked about the note.

"Weel, laddie, seems an alert citizen found a bloody knife in a gutter aboot a block away from the murder scene. 'E were kind enough to turn it over ta the local copper on the beat. Would ya like to come have a look see?"

Pitt smiled. "Seems the proper thing to do since we only have one carriage and we will be going to the Yard first."

It was a boning knife, a common kitchen boning knife nine inches long, honed to a fine edge and covered with dark stains. It was resting on a white cloth in the hands of a constable who said as he handed it to MacLeish, "The coroner says it is human blood but beyond that, it is impossible to tell if it comes from the victim."

Pitt took a close look. On one side of the tang was stamped the word, *Turner* and on the other, *Perth*.

MacLeish handed it back to the constable. "Due to the proximity of discovery near the murder, we shall be considerin' it as evidence for now. Tag it as such."

"Yes sir. Will there be anything else?"

"Nae, lad, nowt now. Off wi' ya."

Pitt took his pipe from his pocket, tamped it, then put a vespa to it. Over the flame and smoke, he asked, "Did you notice the tang?"

"Aye, laddie. It came from Scotland. Shouldnae be surprised…if we are dealin' wi' the Glasgow Horror, that is."

Pitt was silent for a moment, puffing, light blue smoke rising from his pipe. "Well now, Mac, that is the crux of the matter is it not? *If* we are dealing with the Glasgow Horror? And I think not. Asking why I think so will not bring an answer. Tis not that I have one and decline to share it. What I have are questions and conjecture. To my mind, the absence of vital facts leads only to theory and suspicion, neither of which are helpful for the moment. Best perhaps that I retire to my own rooms and think about it."

MacLeish laughed. "A three pipe problem?"

"I'm sure Mr. Holmes would appreciate that comment," replied Pitt, smiling, "but yes, I think you're right. At least three pipes and a small glass of highland malt might be just what is needed. If my speculations are in any way fruitful, I will share them with you."

"Aye, laddie, tha' would be nice."

On his way back to his boarding house, Pitt stopped long enough to send a lengthy telegram to a friend in Glasgow asking for information that he hoped would eliminate at least one point of conjecture. It dealt with the question he wanted to put to Miss MacLaurin when they were interrupted by the constable. When they arrived at 22 Baker Street, he dismissed Fin for the day but asked that he stop by in the morning to see if he was needed.

Mrs. Keating, in flour spotted apron, greeted him as he entered the foyer. "Are you hungry, Mr. Pitt?"

"I wasn't until you asked," he said, smiling.

"Well, if you wait a moment, you can take a ham sandwich up with you. Would you like some tea?"

"Tea would be fine, thank you."

"Come into the kitchen, then. It will only be a moment while I heat the water."

Five minutes later, Pitt was in his sitting room at his desk devouring a thick ham sandwich, sipping a cup of Assam tea, and trying to put his thoughts in order about the case at hand. In reality, it did pose a serious problem. Not the case itself; he had given his imagination full rein and in spite of the similarity, did not believe it was the Glasgow Horror of long ago. No, the problem was that he had two other pressing cases and if the Glasgow Horror incident was not cleared up in a day or two, it was evident he would reluctantly have to leave it to MacLeish.

One of his open cases involved a forger who was crossing checks in outlying districts to City of London banks. He was convinced he knew who it was and was certain the man lived in Paddington. The other involved a forger as well, but in this case, it was forging of obscure art works. The problem was that his arts forger lived in Shoreditch, miles from Paddington and he could not be in two places at once. Three, now, counting the Glasgow situation. Luckily, the check forger had been quiet for a week and he had employed two of Sherlock Holmes Baker Street boys to keep tabs on the art forger. But he was certain it would give him no more than two days to solve the murder of Celia MacLaurin.

He rose, went to his coat hanging on a peg near the door, and removed pipe and tobacco pouch from an outside pocket. Next, he went to the sideboard, poured himself three fingers of whiskey in a tall glass, added a bit of water from the gasogene and then settled into a chair in front of the fireplace to think through what he knew about Celia's murder. The sequence of events was easy enough…Two letters, purportedly from the person who had murdered their mother, produce fear in the sisters and Celia in particular. They are urged by their aunt to take holiday in London. They arrive in the city, take rooms and on their fifth night here, Celia goes out alone to get tea and is murdered less than a block from where they are staying.

Pitt was convinced that answers to the questions raised by the chain of events would provide the solution. After all these years, he found it hard to believe the Glasgow Horror had returned to his murderous habits, but if so, how did the he know where they were staying? How did he know one of the women would go out to buy tea? First and foremost was who wrote the letters? The question of who wrote them, of course begs the question of why? And it was at that point that he drifted off to sleep.

He awoke to the sound of tapping at his door and managed a croaking, "Yes, who is it?" as he rose from the chair. The combination of whiskey and a half bowl of tobacco before drifting off had dried his throat and he was in need of a drink of water or some tea.

Mrs. Keating entered carrying a tray with a hot pot of tea and a fresh cup. "A message from your police friend has come. The boy who brought it knocked at your door but left the note with me when he had no answer. I thought you might be taking a nap but could use a spot of tea at waking."

"Mrs. Keating, you're truly a wonder. Either a mind reader or magician, I care not which, and tea is just the ticket."

She sat the tray on his desk and turned to go. "It was just a half hour ago the boy was here. Supper will be ready in an hour or a bit less. Will you join us downstairs or would you like me to bring something up?"

"Oh, I'll come downstairs, thank you."

He sat at his desk, poured myself a cup of tea, opened the envelope from MacLeish and read the note. *"Miss MacLaurin's aunt arriving Euston Station on the sleeper from Glasgow in the morning. Bell will meet her and take her to see her niece at the location we visited today. If you would care to join us, we should be there about nine of the o'clock. MacLeish."*

Well, he certainly would care to join them. He was convinced the aunt was pivotal in this case but the fact that she was in Scotland and arriving on the morrow resolved nothing and simply raised more questions. It had, in fact, created substantial problems with the theory he held for this case. Unless…But conjecture would get him nowhere at this point. He had hoped for a response from his friend in Glasgow but it was now late and an answer would probably not arrive till morning.

"Nothing for it then," he said aloud, setting the note aside. He finished his tea, selected a pipe from his rack, filled it with Arcadia and headed downstairs for supper. The aroma of curry and spices wafting from the kitchen met him half way down, informing him that Mrs. Keating had prepared one of her Indian dishes this evening. Curried mutton with rice, if he was not mistaken. He wasn't, but the apple tart with clotted cream for desert was an unexpected and pleasant surprise.

Afterwards, puffing on his pipe, he returned to his rooms, glanced again at the note from MacLeish and decided to put it all aside in favor of a whiskey, a book, and a bowl or two of tobacco. He would have enjoyed discussing the matter with Dr. Watson over a game of chess, but the good doctor was out of the city for a few days, visiting the Sussex Downs and looking at property with Holmes. He was glad he asked Fin to stop by in the morning, though only God and Fin knew what time he would arrive. Generally it would be before eight o'clock but if Fin woke at five…

He was up betimes in the morning, completed his toilet, breakfasted, and was enjoying his first pipe of the day when there was a knock at the door. It was Mrs. Keating's houseboy.

"Mornin' sor. They be a cab waitin' tae front. A mister Fin, or so 'e says. 'E's 'avin a cuppa an' said 'e would be ready when you be."

"Thank you, Daniel. Tell Mister Fin I'll be right down."

He donned an old tweed jacket and soft wool cap, picked two pipes from his rack and a full roll-up pouch from the sideboard sill. One pipe went in each of two outside pockets and he slipped the tobacco pouch to an inside one. Almost as an afterthought, he picked up his heavy, worn blackthorn as he walked out the door and down the stairs.

Fin was conversing with Mrs. Keating as Pitt came out the front door and down the short flight of stairs to the kerb.

"Tha were a right fine cuppa, ma'am, and I thank ye for it," said Fin, as he handed an empty cup to Pitt's landlady. "Where we off ta this morning, Gov?"

"Same house as yesterday morning, Fin, but without a stop at the Yard."

Pitt opened the hansom door, stepped up to enter the cab, and as he did so, Mrs. Keating asked, "Will you be home for supper this evening?"

"I certainly hope so, but if I'm unable, I'll try to get word to you. Why? Is there something special this evening?"

"Daniel is with us two years today and I thought I'd bake a cake…"

"Special enough. I'll be here."

Pitt climbed into the cab, closed the door and stayed on the pedestrian side. Pulling a pipe from his pocket, he proceeded to fill and light it as he settled back in the corner to watch London roll by. Daniel was an interesting story. How, exactly, Mrs. Keating came by him, Pitt did not know, but one day he appeared like magic at the house and had taken over running errands and doing general chores. He had been about seven then and obviously a street urchin but how it was that Mrs. Keating had acquired him or vise-versa, Pitt never discovered. Mrs. Keating had taught him to read, at least the basics, but the lad had never lost the cockney that pervaded his speech. Pitt would definitely try to be home in time for cake.

They were soon in front of the same house as the day before and as Pitt was stepping from the cab, he asked Fin to wait at the end of the block. His knock was answered by Tom, the same constable who had been on duty the previous day and as he nodded recognition of Pitt, he said, "Inspector MacLeish is in with the young lady. Inspector Bell has not arrived as yet."

Joshua pocketed his pipe and tapped lightly on the door before entering the sitting room. MacLeish was at the table sipping a cup of tea and Fiona was sitting in a wingback a few feet away, facing the inspector. She looked better this morning, more composed and some color had returned to her cheeks. He removed his cap and set his blackthorn against the wall behind the door.

"Good morning, Mac. Good morning, Miss MacLaurin."

"Fiona, please, Mr. Pitt. I've just asked the inspector to do the same."

"Fiona it is, then, and I'm Joshua. Or if you prefer, just Pitt."

"I like Joshua. It will be Joshua. There's tea in the pot under the cozy if you would like some. And please feel free to smoke your pipe."

"Thank you, I will." He poured himself a cup of tea and looked questioningly at the inspector.

"Aye, laddie, Fiona an' me was just talkin' aboot tae weather an' 'ow nice it has been. Cannae expect it ta continue, though. We are expectin' Mr. Bell momentarily an' I've told Fiona that her aunt will be arrivin' with 'im."

It was obvious to Pitt that MacLeish was not going to broach the subject of the sister's death just yet, preferring to wait perhaps until the aunt was present. They didn't have long to wait. Within minutes, Pitt heard the bell at the door and then voices in the hallway. The sitting room door opened and in walked Inspector Bell followed by a rather striking woman. Not striking in the sense of beauty, but in size. She was taller than Bell and no more than two inches less than Pitt's height of almost six feet. Twelve stone if an ounce, he thought, and not running to fat. She had a full face and a pug nose that seemed turned a bit to one side as if broken once and not properly set. When she removed her scarf, Pitt could see a few flecks of grey beginning to show in her hair but it was not unattractive.

After giving Fiona a hug and a kiss on the cheek, she was introduced around. Given her size, Pitt expected a voice to go with it but was surprised at its softness and the refined Glasgow burr that accompanied it. She sat next to Fiona, and MacLeish poured her a cup of tea as he introduced himself and Joshua. Though it was obvious to Pitt, MacLeish was as surprised as anyone at the large presence of Aunt Maude Wallace but in serving the tea, he succeeded in covering it up. Having poured, he sat back in his chair. "So, you came in on the sleeper from Glasgow, ma'am. I 'ope twer a fair trip."

"Aye, Inspector, it was decent enough though I can't say as I got much sleep. This tragedy kept rising to the top of my mind. Couldnae get shed of it."

"Weel, tis good you be here for tae lass' sake." He paused a moment to put a match to his pipe and Pitt leaned forward.

"How is it you heard of the tragedy, ma'am?"

She looked square at Pitt and for the first time he saw a spark of intelligence and cunning in her eyes.

"And who might you be again, young man?"

"Pitt…Joshua Pitt. A private agent not in the employ of Scotland Yard but I responded to the personal your nieces put in a newspaper." Not said was they had no time to collect the response before Celia was murdered.

She turned to Fiona and in a voice that had a slight edge, said, "What sort of personal did you place?"

"It was Celia's idea," said Fiona, her eyes cast down at her teacup. "She was terrible fearful of the Glasgow Horror and thought we should seek help."

Aunt Maude continued looking at Fiona for a few seconds, then turned back to Pitt. "I read it in the morning paper. There had been no word from Fiona and so I sent two telegrams saying I would be coming to London; one to Scotland Yard and one to Fiona, though at the time, I knew not that Fiona was staying here."

MacLeish removed the pipe from his mouth. "We felt it best tha' she shouldnae be stayin' at her lodgings for a few days till we sorted this out."

"I am sure you know what is best in these circumstances, Inspector, but I was thinking perhaps Fiona should return to Glasgow with me…"

"Tis nowt tha' we be wi'out feelings ma'am but for a few days at least, I'm tinkin' it best she stay here. We would be 'appy tae help you find temporary lodgings for a few days if you plan tae stay in London."

"Why could I not stay here with Fiona?"

"Tis the rules, ma'am. Ta Yard wouldnae permit it."

"In that case, I will find lodgings on my own. I am familiar with London and have stayed here on numerous occasions."

"Very well, Ma'am. Please be kind enough tae inform us where twill be in case we need to contact you."

At that, MacLeish rose and Pitt took it as a signal they were leaving. As they reached the door, MacLeish turned back to the women. "Ta constable will see to you 'avin a cab when you want one. Just ask 'im."

"Thank you Inspector. Good day."

They paused on the steps outside as Pitt relit his pipe. MacLeish did the same and over the flame said, "Verra quiet in there, were ya not, laddie?"

"Thinking…Trying to make sense of it all and not being very successful."

Inspector Bell stepped to the kerb. "I'll get your man, Fin."

"Hold up a minute," said Pitt. "Mac, I think we should leave Fin here to take Aunt Maude wherever she wants to go. We should be able to get a hansom at the end of the block to take you back to the Yard and me to my rooms."

"Fin reportin' back tae you, then."

"And to you, of course, unless there is naught to report."

"I be takin' it ya didnae care for 'er."

"No, but damme if I can say why. Too many pieces and no common thread to connect them, leastways not yet."

"If ya 'ave some thoughts, lad, sharin' would be appreciated."

"I do but it is all theory and conjecture at this point with no foundation in fact, though certain facts may be forthcoming soon. Today, I hope. In the meantime, I will tell you this: I believe the solution to this hideous crime may close to home, at least in a manner of speaking. If I receive any information or discover something on my own hook, I will let you know immediately."

"Fair enough, lad. Now let us talk wi' Fin an' then find us a coach."

Pitt was just starting up the stairs to his rooms when his landlady came through the dining room with a folded telegram in her hand. "This arrived whilst you were out, Mr. Pitt."

He took it, saw that it was from his friend in Glasgow and lengthy. "Thank you Mrs. Keating. Would you be so kind as to brew a wee pot of tea for me?"

"I'll bring it up in about five minutes and I have some freshly baked cinnamon scones as well…"

"You are a delight, Mrs. Keating, truly a delight. Thank you."

Upon entering his sitting room, he took the two pipes and tobacco pouch from his pocket and placed them on his desk next to the telegram, then hung up his coat. He unfolded the telegram and began to read while absentmindedly filling one of the pipes.

> *Joshua—As you know, wills are a matter of public record and it was without difficulty I was able to peruse the original of Mr. MacLaurin. Copies are not permitted, however, nor is one permitted to take any written notes. Though not a lengthy document, I read it through several times to be sure I could remember the particulars. Mr. MacLaurin's estate, including all financial holdings, were placed in trust with the Bank of Scotland to be managed by one Maude Wallace for the benefit of his two daughters. They are to receive full ownership of all property and funds at age twenty-two to be shared equally. In the event that both would decease prior to age twenty-two, the estate would revert to the Maude Wallace referred to above. There were two bequests for small amounts to local charities but the gist of it is what I have related here. If there is additional assistance needed, please feel free to contact me. Best wishes, Benton*

He leaned back in his chair and was just lighting his pipe when Mrs. Keating knocked and then entered carrying a tray with teapot, and two scones on a plate. She sat it on the corner of his desk. "The scones are still warm. Will you be here for supper, then?"

He thought for a moment, then laid his pipe on the desk. "I think not. This telegram means I'll have to see Inspector MacLeish yet again today. I expect Fin will be here in an hour or so. When he arrives, please send him up."

"That I will, sir, though he will probably beg a cuppa from me first."

Pitt smiled. "I expect so. Well, send him up with a cuppa, then."

The hot Assam tea was a counterpoint to the sweet cinnamon scones and they made a delicious combination. He was tempted to go downstairs for another but decided against it and relit his pipe instead. Then he reread the telegram. It confirmed what he suspected and he now had a starting point for his hitherto unfounded speculations. Intuition and imagination did the rest. Staring at his fireplace, slowly puffing on his pipe, he mentally noted his suppositions.

He began with his disbelief that the Glasgow Horror had returned after such a long absence. It was possible, of course, but highly unlikely, and even more so because the young women had been specifically targeted. To his knowledge, the Horror had been a random stalker and killer. He had immediately suspected someone close to Celia and Fiona and now knew the one person who would gain from their deaths was the aunt, Maude Wallace. Suspecting the aunt posed questions and suppositions, however. Why would Maude suggest a trip to London, putting the sisters out of reach, as it were? The fact that Celia had been murdered defied the question, of course, but if Maude was in Glasgow at the time, it implied an accomplice willing to commit murder. Could her husband have secretly returned from where he had been for years? If not him, who? And he could not rule out the possibility that Celia had been murdered by a low life simply after her purse, but the coincidence seemed too great. He would have to ask MacLeish if her purse had been taken or at least turned out. The knife found one street away from the scene also pointed to Scotland and though he had no proof it was the knife used on Celia, he, like MacLeish, had assumed that it was. He still had more questions than answers and to paraphrase Mr. Holmes, it is here that we come into those realms of conjecture where even the most logical mind may be at fault.

If the motive was money, as he assumed, he could only imagine two reasons for it: the estate had been secretly mismanaged or money squandered and Maude feared discovery which could lead to a criminal charge; or what he thought most likely, simple self preservation prompted by fear. Fiona had mentioned no other source of income for Maude and the fact that she would soon be penniless might have driven her to take drastic action. He needed answers…

His thoughts wandered away from the case, or at least the questions he had posed to himself. How strange, that his involvement in this whole affair had begun with coffee and perusal of the agony columns in a newspaper. Had he not chosen to take a walk and in the process, lost track of time…

He had smoked his pipe down to dottle and ash and was absently cleaning out the bowl when a thought suddenly occurred to him. Newspaper! Trains! What if…? A whole chain of events was forming in his mind and even without proven detail, he was certain he was correct. It was imperative he send another telegram to Benton in Glasgow, and quickly. He finished cleaning his pipe, placed it in the rack, selected an large bent Peterson, filled it with a Gawith Flake, but left it unlit as he sat as his desk and composed his note to Benton. Finished, he sat back and lit his pipe while reading what he had written. He was certain that Celia's murder had been committed by Maude Wallace. Now all he had to do was prove it.

There was a knock at the door and a voice from the hallway said, "Tis Fin, Gov. Ta missus gave me a cuppa an' said ya wanted ta see me."

"Come in. Door's open." Pitt smiled. To Fin, every woman over forty years old was a "missus".

Pitt walked to the sideboard. "Would you like a wee drop of whisky to sweeten your tea?"

"I would Gov, but truth be, my belly has been actin' up an' tother than half pint of beer now an' then, I've laid off the stuff."

Pitt poured himself a small one, added some water, and motioned to the chairs in front of the fireplace.

After they were seated, Pitt asked, "So...Did you take your fare round to find lodgings?"

"Aye, but that were strange, Gov."

"How so?"

"I were expectin' 'er to ask about rooms to let but she just gave me an address on Carting Lane an tha's where I took 'er. 'Nother funny thing—when we gets there, I helps her out of the cab an' 'ands 'er bag to 'er, she tips me fair an' then walks right into the house wi'out a ring o' ta bell or a knock."

Pitt sat up straight. "Carting Lane. Near Savoy Street, is it not?"

"Aye. Three streets off, maybe."

"Tell me, was her bag heavy?"

"Nay, light as a feather it were."

"Fin, we have work to do and I expect I'll be needing your services till late tonight. First, we are off to Scotland Yard but I'll need to stop on the way to send a telegram. Later, we will pay a visit to the Euston Station. Can you get word to your missus you will be late? Midnight, I expect."

"Aye. I can send a message w' one o' ta drivers when we get ta Yard."

Pitt entered MacLeish's office without knocking but finding it empty was about to go looking when Inspector Bell entered.

"Is MacLeish in the building?"

"He's with the Superintendent. Can I help you with something, Mr. Pitt?"

"I know we do not always see eye to eye on some matters, Inspector, but it is crucial that Mrs. Wallace be watched. If you have a man free to do that, I have Fin outside who will take him to her rooming house. If you will take my word as to the importance of the matter, I will explain in detail when MacLeish returns."

Bell looked at him intently for a moment, then went to the next door office and returned with a large, well built, plain clothes officer; a man who had Ireland and pugilism written on his face. "Mr. Pitt, this Paddy Reilly. Mr. Pitt will tell who you will be watching and provide you with a description. He has a hansom waiting outside."

Pitt described Mrs. Wallace to Reilly and told him it was extremely important that he not be seen if she left the boarding house but imperative that he note any shop or house that she might visit. He should also note any visitors to the boarding house. A simple description of them would be sufficient for now. If he was not relieved by midnight, he could call it a night and go home. Reilly repeated the instructions almost word for word and then left.

"Seems a good man," said Pitt.

"He is that…As you know, I do not hold much with private inquiry agents as you are, but seein' as you have been of assistance several times in the past, I have taken you at your word as to the importance of this matter. Inspector MacLeish will be along in a few moments and I'll be interested to hear what you have to say. In the meantime, would you like a cuppa?"

"Yes I would, Mr. Bell, very much so."

"Be back in a tic," said Bell and walked out the door.

Bell was all copper; very protective of his turf and not as easy going as MacLeish but a fellow you could entrust your life to, which may have been his only endearing quality. Pitt knew of no one that called him friend, including MacLeish. True to his word, he was back in a moment carrying three cups of tea, two that he sat on MacLeish's desk.

"The brown one has sugar in it and the white one is plain."

As Pitt picked up the white cup, MacLeish came through the door and walked to the far side of his desk where he sat down and stared at the teacup. "Weel, lads, yon Superintendent is on a real tear over this MacLaurin murder. 'E says we need 'positive results' afore newspapers start splashing Glasgow Horror all over ta front page, as if they havenae already. Ta *Times* an' *Guardian* havenae done it but some local rags 'ave." It suddenly dawned on him that it was Pitt standing on the other side of the desk sipping tea. "An' what brings Mr. Pitt here today? Out of tobacco?"

"I know who murdered Celia MacLaurin."

The sip of tea MacLeish was taking was blown back into the cup and he simply stared at Pitt over the rim. "Say tha' agin, lad."

"I know who murdered Celia MacLaurin and I think I know how it was done, but I need some help to prove it."

"Who?"

"Maude Wallace."

"Ach, lad…Bullocks! She were in Glasgow."

"I cannot believe that and I will tell you why." Pit proceeded to lay out step by logical step why and how Mrs. Wallace planned to murder both sisters. He finished up by asking if there was someone who could draw a likeness of her from a description supplied by himself, Bell, and MacLeish.

MacLeish was looking at Pitt with his mouth open. Pitt laughed. "Mac, if you would put a pipe in your mouth it would fill the gap."

MacLeish ignored the jibe and said, "By God, lad, I be tinkin' you may be right." He looked questioningly at Bell who came over to the desk and set his cup down. "Angus, I think he is right but we have no proof."

Pitt fished in his pockets for pipe and tobacco pouch. "I sent a second telegram to a friend in Glasgow asking when the story of Celia's murder first appeared in any of the local papers. I expect an answer yet today but will bet that it did not appear till the later editions. If that is true, then Mrs. Wallace lied about seeing the notice in the morning edition of the newspaper. It means she already knew, and the reason she knew is because she did it. It also means she was not in Glasgow the night of the murder, but that she was here in London."

"But she arrived on the sleeper," said Bell. "I was there to meet her."

"Certainly she did, but that was because she took the night train to Glasgow after she murdered Celia. She was just a short distance from the Embankment and could easily have gotten a carriage to Euston in time to catch the train. The murder occurred between nine o'clock and half past if your guess about the dried blood is correct, and we have no reason to doubt it because the body was discovered at ten o'clock. The night train to Glasgow departs at eleven o'clock. She arrives in Glasgow, waits till late afternoon to send two telegrams and then catches the sleeper back to London that evening."

"Jasus!" Bell sat down in a chair next to MacLeish's desk. "But why London? Why convince the sisters to come to London on holiday when it would have been simpler to do it in Glasgow?"

Pitt was lighting his pipe but between puffs he said, "Conjecture…on my part, of course…but I think distance…was the reason." He took a final puff and blew out the match. "One other thing…was Celia's purse found with her and was there money in it?"

Bell set his cup on MacLeish's desk. "It was found under the body and held a couple of quid and change."

"That rules out robbery as a motive and makes it intended murder, pure and simple." Pitt set his pipe on the desk and picked up his cup. "The circumstance begs the question of how Mrs. Wallace knew Celia would be going out to buy tea that night and I think we may discover she did not know. I think she was keeping close watch on the sisters and the appearance of Celia on the street that night presented her with an unexpected opportunity to carry out the deed. In reality, she may simply have planned to *drop in* on the sisters to see how they were doing. It would not have surprised them. How she intended to murder them both in their rooms is open to conjecture but a sleeping drug in their tea would be sufficient to prepare them for the knife."

MacLeish pulled a pipe from his pocket, checked to see that it still had tobacco in the bowl and then put a match to it. "My God, lad, but ye 'ave a fertile mind! Is there ever a ting that puzzles ya?"

"Yes. Why people do what they do, but I will leave that to doctors who specialize in that sort of thing. I have enough on my plate."

A constable was brought in who drew a reasonable likeness of Mrs. Wallace from the descriptions given. He had just finished when a clerk came in to tell them that Fin had arrived back from dropping of the watcher and would be at the stand at the end of the block. MacLeish asked Pitt what he intended to do with the picture.

"Wait till late evening and then go to Euston Station and query the ticket sellers as to whether they have seen this woman before and when. Her height alone should make her stand out but the drawing will help. If a railway clerk can confirm she bought a ticket to Glasgow the night of the murder…"

"Then we will have her," broke in Bell.

"We will certainly have another piece of strong evidence but no way to place her on Savoy Street at the time Celia was murdered."

"But if we confront her with what evidence we have?"

"She does not strike me as one who would readily confess. No, I think we need more and what I have in mind would involve Fiona. The problem is that I am not sure she is up to participating in a scheme that would entrap her aunt. After all, the woman did raise them after their father passed away."

MacLeish stood and stretched. "Wha' 'ave ya in mind, lad?"

"We could move Fiona back to her lodgings tomorrow and let it be known to Mrs. Wallace that we think the motive for Celia's death was robbery. Say her purse was missing. Mrs. Wallace knows she did not take it but who is to say someone did not come along afterwards and see it as easy pickings? The story would throw any suspicion away from her and she would accept it. I think, however, she would not now go so far as to attempt murder in Fiona's rooms. Doing so, might implicate her in some way, or at least she would think it possible. No…what we need is a brave young lady willing to venture out on the streets after dark to visit her aunt."

"Oh, laddie, you will no be getting tha' young lady tae streets after dark even if she would agree wi' wha' ya say."

"I know that. But it would only be necessary for her to convince Mrs. Wallace that she would set out for her aunt's rooms at a certain time and on a certain route. It will be dark, and if we could substitute one of the women warders from Newgate Prison—one who is similar in build to Fiona..."

"By God, Mr. Pitt," said Bell, smiling, "it is probably a good thing you have chosen this side of the law than the other. Hard telling what we would have to put up with if you decided being a cracksman was your lot in life."

Pitt smiled back. "I will be sure to let you know if I change direction. In the meantime, I would like to visit alone with Fiona this afternoon. I think it best you not be there as it might be overwhelming for her to be confronted with her aunt's involvement by three men, two of whom are with the police. I fear that under those circumstances she might reluctantly agree and then have second thoughts later. That would not do. The fact that I am a fellow Scot and the one who responded to Celia's personal, just might just carry the day. And I have a reason for dropping in to see her; I left my blackthorn walking stick behind the door of the sitting room when last there."

"Was that planned as well, Mr. Pitt?"

"No, Mr. Bell, it was not," he said, smiling. "It was purely accident. I plain forgot it when we walked out."

"Well, it is nice to know you have some human failings."

"I think I'll be on my way, gentlemen, and plan to return on the morrow at about nine o'clock. By then, we should know three things at least: which edition it was in Glasgow that first carried the story; whether Mrs. Wallace returned to Glasgow the night of the murder; and if Fiona will cooperate. Good day to you both."

He found Fin outside and as he climbed into the hansom, directed him to go first to his rooms on Baker Street and then to the boarding house in Soho and then settled back into a corner. He was tired and almost wished he were headed back to his rooms to stay for a nap. Ah well...later.

Mrs. Keating was sweeping the front steps as they pulled to the kerb and she came over to the cab pulling a folded piece of paper from her apron. "This telegram came for you just five minutes ago, Mr. Pitt."

He took it and read it quickly through. It was from Benton and confirmed what he had suspected about a newspaper report of Celia's murder. No article in any of the local newspapers in the morning and only one short wire report in *The Scotsman* late edition that evening. It wasn't till the following morning, the morning Mrs. Wallace was arriving in London, that the local newspapers in Glasgow carried the entire report.

"Thank you, Mrs. Keating. One moment while I get something, Fin, then we are off to Soho."

He ran up the stairs to his sitting room, collected the first telegram from Benton, and was back down in less that a minute. Fin whipped up the horse and they were on their way.

He was met at the door by Tom and grinned as he asked if Tom was living here now.

Tom chuckled. "Seems that way, sir. Are the inspectors coming along?"

"No, they remained at the Yard. I'm to see the young lady alone."

"Hmmm...I see...Would you like some tea?"

"Yes—Wait a minute. Do you have anything stronger in the house?"

"Some whiskey, and I believe, a bottle of Sherry."

"Both, then. Is Miss MacLaurin in her room?"

"The sitting room, sir."

"Good. I'll see my way to the sitting room and you can bring the drinks along in a few minutes."

He tapped at the door and then entered. She was sitting in a high backed chair in the window alcove with an open book on her lap and looked up as he came in.

After taking a chair opposite and pulling pipe and tobacco from his pocket, he nodded at the book. "What are you reading?"

"Kipling, but try as I might, I cannot seem to concentrate."

"I think that understandable. But I have some things to say to you—difficult things—and I need you to concentrate on what I am saying. Do you think you can do that?"

She nodded. "If it has do with Celia's death, I will do what needs be done."

"Fine, because I'm going to need your help."

At that moment, Tom came in carrying a tray with two decanters, glasses, and a water carafe, and set it down on a small side table near them. "If you need anything else, Mr. Pitt, I'll be in the pantry off the kitchen."

"Thank you, Tom, this will do nicely for now."

He poured a stiff whiskey and water for himself, a small sherry for Fiona that he handed to her without asking if she wanted one, and then paused to take a sip of his drink and light his pipe.

"What I'm going to tell you cannot be discussed further with anyone but myself or Mr. Bell and Mr. MacLeish. No talking it over with your aunt, or even Tom here; particularly with your aunt as you will see."

She nodded agreement and he began at the beginning with his first suspicions and proceeded to logically identify each incriminating point against Mrs. Wallace. When he was finished, she was crying softly, but he handed her both telegrams he had received from Benton. She took a handkerchief from her sleeve, wiped her eyes, and then slowly read the telegrams before raising her eyes to Pitt.

"What you say must be true, Joshua, but I can still hardly believe it. Aunt Maude raised us, took care of us. How could she possibly do something like this?"

"That is probably the one thing I cannot respond to. People do strange things when they feel threatened and I assume she did, though I have no foundation for that assumption."

"We would have certainly provided for her, Celia and I, just as she did for us, though I do not think we ever discussed it with her."

"It may be more than simple provision, Fiona. If you have never had an accounting of your father's estate, it is entirely possible Mrs. Wallace has been taking substantial sums from the account for some purpose. If that were the case, it would be fear of discovery that could prompt the terrible action she plotted. Her reasons, however, are not as important at this time as is proving our case against her for the murder of your sister. In order to do that, we need your assistance. Has your aunt visited you today?"

"No, but I expect her later this evening."

Pitt went on to explain that they wanted her to move back to her lodgings on the following morning. She was to tell her aunt that the police thought Celia's death was an isolated incident, a robbery gone bad. She was to say the police were working on leads and wished her to remain in London for several more days in hopes that she might be able to identify someone seen in the neighborhood. Most important would be telling her aunt she wished to visit her for tea late tomorrow evening about half past eight; that she wasn't afraid to go out at night because it wasn't the Glasgow Horror who had killed her sister. Pitt paused and relit his pipe.

"Do you think you can do that, Fiona?"

"I must...For Celia, I must. But what if she attacks me on the way there?"

"You will be watched closely by myself and several other police officers on your way there, but we feel it would be unlikely for her to make any attempt so early. It will most likely occur on your way back to your rooms and we have provided for that. Just a half block from your aunts lodging house, a female warder from Newgate will take your place and you will come with us. Your replacement will be ready for any eventuality."

For the first time since his arrival, she smiled. "This sounds like one of those thrupenny mysteries bought at newsstands."

He smiled back. "It does, but sadly, this is real life and the consequences are real. Do you think you can carry it off?"

"Yes, certainly. It will be for Celia, will it not?"

"It will. I am afraid I have to leave now, as I have several other related tasks to carry out, but I will see you tomorrow evening. On my way out, I will ask Tom to come in and pick up the tray."

"Thank you, Joshua, for coming to talk with me. I am glad it was you and not the police inspectors who were here earlier." She smiled again. "I think they may have been too official."

"You may be right." On his way out, he picked up his blackthorn so conveniently forgotten behind the sitting room door.

Outside and before he climbed into the carriage he stopped to tap ash and dottle from his pipe and refill it with Arcadia. "I think we should go back to my place, Fin, at least for a couple of hours before we go to Euston Station. I told Mrs. Keating I would not be home for supper but she should be able to put together a sandwich for both of us. That alright with you?"

"Truth told, Gov'nor, I were getting a wee bit hungry. A sandwich 'ud fine."

"My place it is, then," he said as he climbed aboard.

Mrs. Keating managed two roast beef sandwiches with horseradish on freshly baked bread and sent her boy to the corner pub for a pitcher of beer. They sat at Pitt's desk and Fin was thoroughly enjoying himself to the extent of having a half glass of beer with his meal.

"I don' know why we are doin' all the runnin' about, Gov, and o' course its none o' my affair, but I was curious ta know about the fella I dropped at the woman's lodgings just short after midday. 'E were a hard lookin' fella for sure, an Irish ta boot."

Pitt chucked. "And a copper as well, eh?"

"I dinna know tha' but could guess."

"Well, there is no reason you should not know—at least I cannot think of one offhand." Pitt spent the better part of the next hour telling Fin about the case from the very beginning to what he hoped he would accomplish at Euston Station."

When he finished, Fin said, "Well, if tha' don' beat all, Gov. A puzzlement for certain an' ya solved it. If tha' don' beat all."

"Solved maybe, Fin, but not completely provable as yet. We had better be going. I'll get my jacket and a pipe."

The inside of Euston Station was cavernous with more than a dozen loading platforms still moderately crowded with people waiting on night trains to different destinations. Pitt went to the first ticket agent, stood politely in line and when it was his turn, showed the drawing and described Mrs. Wallace, asking if the agent remembered her from the night in question. No, he didn't. The same at the second the third agents. The fourth, however, knew her immediately.

"Tall, she were. Tall an' built like a Rugby player."

"And she bought a ticket for the Glasgow night train Monday last?"

"She did. But that were the second time I seed her."

"The second time?"

"Aye. The first I seed her were the Friday afore. Bought a ticket for the same train, dint she?"

"Have you seen her since?"

"Nay, just the twice."

"Could I have your name, sir?"

"You a copper?"

"No, private inquiry agent."

"Tha' bein' the case, the name is 'Enry Blaut."

"Thank you Mr. Henry Blaut. You have been a great help."

Pitt had what he wanted. More than he'd hoped, in fact. He could not help but wonder why Mrs. Wallace had traveled to London the Friday before. Perhaps only to look over the lay of the land, so to speak. Then it came to him. Of course…she had brought clothes with her the first time and booked rooms at the boarding house Fin had taken her to after her first visit with Fiona. That was why she walked right into the house without ringing or knocking. That was also why the suitcase was so light—she had brought whatever clothes and toiletries she needed on the first trip. The second suitcase was a sham. He would get MacLeish to confirm it but not just yet. Not till after tomorrow evening.

Tired and drained, he rode back to his rooming house not even making an attempt to light his pipe in the carriage, as was his usual wont. He asked Fin to pick him up at about eight o'clock, bade him goodnight, and went directly to his sitting room. There, he took off his hat and coat, emptied the pockets of pipe and tobacco, turned down the gaslight and went to bed. It had been a long day.

Fin was on time in the morning and they drove straight away to Scotland Yard. MacLeish and Bell were both in and Pitt spent the better part of an hour discussing the second telegram he had received, his interview with the ticket clerk at Euston Station, and the evidence that had so far. Paddy Reilly had reported that only one person, a man, had been seen entering Mrs. Wallace's boarding house but by midnight, he had not come out and Paddy assumed he was a lodger.

Mrs. Wallace, however, had gone out and Reilly admitted the man he had seen entering could have left in the thirty minutes or so that he had been tagging along behind her. He followed her to a general merchandise store and then to a tea shop before she returned to her rooms. There was no sign of any purchase she might have made at the merchandise store but her handbag was large and it could have been in that. She did carry a small packet from the tea shop.

They then spent some time reviewing their plans for that evening and Pitt was introduced to Alice Cornwell, a warder at Newgate who resembled to some degree, Fiona MacLaurin. She was about the same height and weight but with dark hair and totally different facial features. No one thought it would matter much. They would have Fiona wear a headscarf and she could switch scarf and all-weather coat with Alice less than a block from Mrs. Wallace's boarding house. Alice would then make her way slowly along the remaining four streets to Fiona's rooms on Exeter. If any attack was going to take place, they thought it most likely on Savoy or Burleigh, and that is the route Alice would take.

"Now fellows," said MacLeish taking a sip of tea, "ta hitch in ta whole scheme is if Mrs. Wallace gives a pass tae our bait. Wot then?"

Pitt fiddled with his pipe but left it unlit. "We wait a night and do it again but I truly believe she wont pass up the chance. For all she knows, you fellows will give Fiona the go ahead to return to Glasgow in a day or two and Maude Wallace wants the crime to be committed in London. No, I look for her to slip out a minute or two behind Fiona which gives us just seconds, by the way, for Alice and Fiona to switch scarf and coat. There is a narrow alley just half a block from Mrs. Wallace's rooms and no gaslight near. That would be the best place to switch and it would only take a few seconds."

Bell commented there would be a dozen constables in and around the area but keeping out of sight. They agreed to meet a block from Fiona's lodgings at half past seven, then talked for a few minutes more but no one had anything to add to what had already been discussed. Pitt took his leave after saying he would see Fiona late afternoon and if there were any hitch, he would contact MacLeish.

The next three hours he spent checking on his two other cases that were still noticeably quiet. The check forger, he could understand. He'd managed to pass almost three hundred quid in phony paper just three weeks before, but the art forger had been laying low for an even longer period and was due to begin making contacts in the collector community. Harvey and Prong, the two Baker Street lads he had on watch had nothing to report.

Soon after four o'clock found him at Fiona's original boarding house to where she had returned earlier in the day. Aunt Maude had been there two hours earlier and had been quite solicitous from Fiona's account.

"When I said that I would enjoy tea and company late this evening at her place, she voiced no objection but simply said she would stop at the bakery on her way back and buy some cakes to have with tea. Of course, I had already sent a message to her by way of Tom that the police suspected robbery in Celia's death and that I would be moving back to my old lodgings. Perhaps she just accepted that."

"Perhaps," said Pitt. He did not voice it but thought it more likely that any objection would keep Fiona off the streets that night. "What I am going to tell you is the plan for this evening and I assure you, you will be accompanied or watched closely every step of the way."

He spent the next half hour telling her of the route she would take to and from her aunt's Carting Lane lodgings, which would be the same. He then noted on a small hand drawn map he had made, the narrow alley was that the clothing switch would be made with the Newgate warder.

"Will you be there, Joshua?"

"Not at the alley, but further along the way. You remember Inspector Bell? He will be with the woman who will don your coat and scarf and stay with you the remainder of the time. You will be quite safe with him."

Upon leaving, he was surprised to discover the weather had changed during his visit. What had been weak sunshine and broken clouds, was now grey overcast and a light rain was falling. There would be fog tonight, he thought…Perfect weather for a murder in the streets of London.

"I am afraid you will be late again tonight, Fin," he said as he entered the carriage. "Can you get word to your missus?"

"I tole 'er this mornin' over tea to spect me when my face shows ta door."

"Back to my place, then. We will see if we can talk Mrs. Keating into a light meal of sorts and then we will return to this area but at the end of the street."

The rain had stopped but Pitt had been right about the fog. It was moderately heavy and the glow of the streetlamps could barely be seen beyond fifty feet. MacLeish, Bell, Alice Cornwell, and two constables were standing just outside the diffused glow of the lamp at the end of the block as Fin pulled to the kerb and Pitt stepped to the cobbles.

"Weel lad, tis a night for mayhem, I tink," said MacLeish, putting a match to his pipe.

"Right you are, Mac and it concerns me. I fear we might lose sight of Miss MacLaurin in this pea soup."

"Aye, meself as well, so we added two extra men along ta way. Ta girl wont be out o' sight ta whole trip."

"There is a small pocket park at Savoy Place and I thought I would station myself there. Half way along the route I think."

"Aye, aboot half. You take one end and meself will be at tother. He turned to Bell and the warder. "Better be off tae be in place afore she comes along."

Pitt took a pipe from his pocket, tamped down the tobacco that was already in the bowl and lit it. "Fin can take us to the park, then drive round the corner to be out of sight. Tis going to be a long night, Mac, and a damp one."

He was in place behind some tall bushes twenty feet off the street for about ten minutes when he saw Fiona emerge from the dark and fog into the glow of a streetlamp. She was moving quickly and glancing in all directions as walked. No sooner had she passed in front of Pitt's position, another figure ambled into the light as if out for an evening stroll. It was Paddy Reilly, following just far enough behind to be out of sight but close enough to reach her in seconds. Pitt felt more comfortable knowing Reilly was there and wished Fiona knew.

Twenty minutes passed, then thirty, and having heard no police whistles, he assumed she had arrived at her aunt's rooming house safely. He rested his blackthorn against a bush and was tapping the dottle from his pipe when a figure emerged into the dim glow of the lamp from the opposite direction. It was MacLeish. Pitt tucked his blackthorn under his arm and stepped out from the shrubbery to the edge of the street.

"Ta police runner informs me Miss MacLaurin is tae aunt's place. Twill be another hour or so afore she starts back. A cuppa would be a nice ting."

"When it is over, Mac, when it is over…then we can add a wee dram of whiskey as well. You did not mention Paddy Reilly would be dogging her."

"Aye, weel, I was tinkin' 'e would be a good 'un. Stout enough tae bust tru a brick wall, if I be any measure of 'im.

"He carries the face of a boxer."

"I were told 'e picked up a few quid tha' way afore 'e joined the force but has never talked of it w' me."

They stood smoking their pipes and talking for a bit, then at Pitt's suggestion walked the length of the park and back just to generate some warmth and push back the chill of the fog. After checking his pocket watch and seeing almost an hour had passed, Macleish went back to his post and Pitt took up his place again behind the shrubbery. Long minutes passed…He was about to put his unlit pipe in his mouth when he heard the blast of a police whistle and shouts coming from MacLeish's direction. He turned, took two steps, tripped on an exposed root and fell flat. He hadn't time to brace himself or put a hand out to break the fall and his head snapped forward hitting the hard wet ground. Small streaks of light flashed across his vision but he stumbled to his feet, dizzy and disoriented but resumed moving in the direction of the whistle.

He had gone no more than twenty feet deeper into the park when he heard the sound of running in his direction. Someone was crashing through the bushes and a deep booming voice shouted, "Stop! Police!" There was a small clearing ahead bordered by a stone wall of about five feet high and as Pitt burst into it he could see Maude Wallace, back to the wall, cornered by PC Reilly. Her face was twisted so that Pitt hardly recognized her and she was growling like a cornered beast. In her right hand was a long thin bladed knife and she was slashing back and forth with it in Reilly's direction. He could hear Reilly trying to reason with her, telling her to drop the knife; that she would come to no harm if she dropped the knife. Pitt stopped moving and watched.

She lunged at Reilly, slashing in a long arc that would have opened him all the way across the chest had he still been directly in front of her but with the motion and skill of an experienced boxer he simple moved a few inches out of reach. She pulled the knife back to almost waist level and crouched like a cat waiting to pounce. Pitt saw Reilly shrug his shoulders as if coming to a decision. Reilly feinted to his right, then to his left, and as she straightened to follow his motion, raising the knife to strike out again, he hit her with a left hook between the eyes that would have dropped an ox. She bounced once against the stone wall and collapsed like an empty burlap sack.

Pitt reached him just as he was removing the knife from her hand. It had blood on it as did the sleeve of her coat.

"Did she cut you, Paddy?"

"Not me, but she came up on Alice so quickly she managed to strike once before Alice twisted away and I came on the scene. I were about fifty feet behind Alice and gave out a yell. Twas then the woman took off running an' I gave chase. Almost caught 'er at the edge of the park but she twisted out of my grip. Strong as a bull, she is."

MacLeish and Bell had arrived while he was telling this to Pitt and Reilly turned toward them. "Alice hurt bad?"

"Nay, lad. Bell says she took a long cut from 'er left shoulder an' over 'er collar bone but she be on 'er way to Charing Cross hospital an' should be alright." MacLeish turned his Deitz dark lantern on Pitt. "Fall in the mud, did ya lad?"

Even in the dim light, Pitt could see he was a mess with mud from boots to chest high. He felt his forehead. Mud there too. "Tripped on a root," was all he could think of to say.

Mrs. Wallace was still unconscious but they put darbys on her anyway and carried her to a waiting police wagon. Standing silently next to the wagon when they laid her in was Fiona MacLaurin. She turned to Pitt. "She really intended to kill me, did she not." It was a statement, not a question.

"Yes, she did."

"I think I have you to thank that I'm still alive."

"No…I think you should say a silent prayer of thanks to your dead sister. Had she not place a personal about the Glasgow Horror in the *Times*, I should never have been involved."

"You are a modest man, Mr. Pitt."

"Thank you, but there are some who would disagree. I see Fin coming round the corner with his carriage. Come along and we will take you to your rooms."

From Fiona's boarding house to Baker Street was a short trip and Pitt made no attempt to light a pipe. He said good night to Fin with thanks and a sovereign, slowly climbed the stairs to his sitting room and removed is muddy coat. He poured water in a basin and washed as best he could, thinking that any mud left could wait till the morrow as could cleaning the pipe he had carried that evening.

He selected another pipe from his rack on the sideboard, poured himself at least three fingers of whiskey in a glass and walked to the wingback in front of the fireplace. He took a sip of whiskey, filled his pipe with Arcadia tobacco, lit it and blew out a long stream of smoke. The best part of the day, he thought…The pipe and the whiskey.

END

0-595-31547-X

Made in the USA
Lexington, KY
16 June 2014